A Piece of Peace

A Piece of Peace

OEBooks
Published by OSAAT Entertainment
Pennsylvania

OSAAT Entertainment, P.O. Box 1057
Bryn Mawr, Pennsylvania, 19010-7057

All rights reserved. This work is a work of fiction.

No part of this book may be reproduced or transmitted in any form or by any means, graphic, electronic, or mechanical, including photocopying, recording, taping, or by any information storage retrieval system, without the written permission of the publisher.

First Edition. Fiction

To Contact the Author Visit: www.osaatpublishing.com
Email: rycj@osaatpublishing.com

Copyright © 2011 (RYCJ), A piece of peace.
Cover Design by RYCJ

Library of Congress Control Number: 2010919053

ISBN: 978-0-9827152-5-3
Printed in the United States of America

We're never too old to fall in love,
And it's never too late to forgive.

2012

God Bless

Thank you
Divas

CHAPTER...1

Clifford wouldn't say he was a religious man. He didn't run up to people, stopping them mid sentence to remind them he was five-foot/nine, or decent looking, or black, any more than he sat around reminding everyone that he believed in God. In God he trusted people would look at him and assume these things.

He would say he was a spiritual man however, even if he didn't put this information on full blast either. But then he was a rare breed. He still believed in helping strangers, whether they were indigent or well-off. A person didn't have to be barefoot, missing teeth, and have holes in their pockets before he would reach down and give them a hand. Falling was enough.

But if this sounds like a yawn too good to be true, look out, it is. Clifford had a few socio-paraplegic issues. For one, and two, he never got married and didn't have any children. These were two major issues that didn't sit right with a lot of people, namely his sister Meredith, who he grew up calling Merda.

Take a good guess why he called her that, because he sure wasn't saying. All anyone needed to know was that a long time ago, fifty-one years and some change, he couldn't pronounce her name. But they were even. She called him Satan. She started calling him that the day he came home from the hospital, their mother carrying him in her loving arms. She said he cried too much, and when he got a little older, and was left in her care, she said he got into too much. She said he was too spoiled, too. And she also said she hated him.

But guess what? Merda believed in God. And she told everyone about her beliefs, too. She said she didn't care who didn't care. She wasn't shamed of the Lord she served. God had been good to her, and indeed He had been. Quite a few men serving time in the pen could attest to that. As a matter of fact, it's all they attested to. And as well all it's all they attested to, what they would do to her once they got out, if they ever got out.

But Fine. Let bygones be bygones. It was all water over a bridge. Dirt swept under a rug. Half a county of street hoods dimmed out and deservingly locked up. Now Merda's a saved woman. She ratted on the friends she ran out with, and ran down to Florida a praying woman, hoping one of them didn't in fact get out.

This stuff happened years ago, her running down to Florida, and literally running on both feet, to disappear for a few years she later described as a time when she was finding herself, getting saved she said.

Found! The family found out she was shacking up with a guy running foul like her during *her* lost and found sin-filled years. The new guy was spelling ethical work lumped together in one word. Try fraud. Or try driving up a tree and blaming it on the rich guy who'd rather pay off a poor man purporting to be hurt, rather than having his name dragged through a community rallying against loaded and toasted rich drivers who drove drunk. Merda met this man, Parker, as he was collecting, settling to the tune of a half a million dollars. Two of a kind those two were. Ask anyone who cared about telling the truth, they were a perfect match.

Parker, and all his working parts, moved on to bank-roll the city, adding zeros behind zeros collecting on disability, SSI, workman's comp and the likes, though the man hadn't worked a real job a day in his life.

Cliff hadn't met Parker, who Merda talked up to his mother and other family, calling the bum her savior, or saving grace. Yah, right. Cliff knew exactly what Merda was up to. Both him and his father, Pop's, knew. She was up to her old tricks. She was cleaning Parker out. And true to the last coin she did just that. Cleaned out his trust fund, his pockets, and nearly ruined his good relationship with Uncle Sam before she went to work cleaning out his head. To everyone back home though, she claimed she was helping Parker clean up his act. A small matter of perception he supposed only saints could see.

Cliff wasn't a saint, at least not that kind of saint, one that forgave and forgot a whole lot. He remembered it all, and swore never to forget…as long as he lived. Who could ever ignore, and forget forgive, a sister who treated him the way Merda treated him? He put her high on his unforgivable list, even as he packed up with everyone but his father, and drove down to Florida to witness a whole bunch of firsts in the family.

Call him cynical, or scornful, or what Merda always called him, Satan, but not one prostitute in the family had ever gotten married before. In fact, there had never been a *known* prostitute in the family. Also, they'd never been to a wedding held at the type of courthouse where Merda's wedding ended up taking place. She had sent out the most lovely wedding invitations made of crepe paper and tissue paper, sand and beaches, and the most bizarre thing happened. She got locked up for what no one was saying. Just as they were loading up the vans, Merda was pleading her case to police, trying to get them to believe she was really in Motel Six selling Avon cosmetics. But the police wouldn't buy it. If only the video hadn't picked up her taking money for goods not made by Avon.

It was a big embarrassment to their mother, and Cliff felt plenty sad for Mama, but was a happy prophet otherwise. The swanky invitations and all the lies had him fooled none. He remembered Merda, and knew her style well. The only reason he packed up and ran down to Florida with everyone else, was to hit the beaches Merda described in her many omnificent calls back home. It was the only truth he ever believed coming out of her mouth. Florida was a good place to catch plenty of sunshine…and beauties sunbathing on the beaches.

All accept for an uncle, Uncle Jamison, who went along for the ride for the same reason he had, no one was laughing about Merda's predicament.

"All right now Jameson," that's how Aunt Idell, Mama and Jamison's oldest sister, and Cliff's favorite aunt, pronounced Jamison's name. "You know it's not right laughing at people's pain."

But Jamison tapped him on the leg, ignoring Aunt Idell. "Hey look man, just block me if it look like I'm about to catch the garter." And Jamison doubled over to his knees. "Cause man...ain't nothing I can do with a yard girl," and he howled.

Mama wasn't in the room while all this cutting up was going on. Cliff would have stopped him if she were. He didn't want to hurt Mama's feelings, even if it hurt his feelings seeing how Mama seemed to favor Merda. He respected Mama more than anything, choosing to believe she cared for them in different ways. It wasn't her fault that he thought Merda didn't deserve to be cared for at all. Not by the hateful and crooked way she lived her life, mainly in these early days.

• • •

Merda returned home on the day their mother died. Despite Cliff having called her weeks in advance, when Mama was first put in the hospice, she slid in town with her slimly Parker fifteen hours after Mama was taken off the respirator, and three hours and fifty-nine minutes after she took her last breath.

After all Mama had done for Merda, the many jams she pulled her out of, the love and support she always showed her, and the fact that Mama would screw up the Will, putting in a clause where Merda could end up with the house, and this was the most Mama meant to her. How nice of a sister is that?

Mama had one of them funerals he didn't want to live through twice. Her home-going was nothing like Pop's, who left out like an angel. One day, a few years before Mama went home, and a decade after Merda's wily wedding, he quietly became ill, sleeping more than his usual after 30-years working as a traveling salesman, and quietly went home. Mama just as quietly made funeral arrangements, and Merda just as coolly slipped into town…this being in the days before the Lord recovered most of her. She didn't want everyone knowing she and her saving grace were still going through *some things*, so she slipped in and out of town without much fuss.

Not this time however. Not when it came time to laying their dear mother to rest. Good grief Tampa Bay, Merda marched in the house her old bossy, hostile, unrepentant self. Barging in smelling like fried chicken and a nonstandard fragrance, she hugged and kissed him like she always did—phony, trying to fool him, like he hadn't forgotten her old tricks. The huggaroo was one of her oldest tricks. This was the hug where he would be thinking nice things about her, wanting to believe she changed…when slam! She'd bring out the sword and chop off another piece of his heart.

Sure enough, right after the hugs and kisses, she pulled out the sword and again slammed into his heart. Mama wouldn't want this, and Mama wouldn't want that, along with one more errant tirade that turned his grief into a tumulus spade. "…And what are your plans Satan, now that Mama is gone!?!"

How about first getting Mama in the ground, where her soul could rest, and then *let's hope to whoever you pray to*, I don't have to bury you right alongside Mama.

Great nerve. *What were his plans*? The real question was, what were her plans? Forget Mama for the time being. He put a lot of work into the home; Brazilian cherry hardwood floors, honeycombed ceilings, spare rooms and bathrooms, he wasn't going nowhere. This was his home, the only home he had known. The home Pop paid off ten years after buying it, something a gypsy would have no respect for.

He didn't care if she *looked* cleaned up. Much older, and much wiser his foot. The beady evil-high eye was gone, but shifty bedeviled eyes had taken its place. And it really got beneath his skin looking at all that extra gel she had worked into her scalp. Obviously, she not long ago had been in to see a beautician, likely while he was busy working on the obituary she wanted corrected; at his expense since it was his mistake he left Parker's name off the program.

That's how Mama's funeral started. Hostile. Merda yapping on about Parker and this obituary, and him hoping to keep the peace until after the funeral. After the funeral he would be more than happy to put both her name and Parker's name in an obituary. Right there on the cover. He would even go out of his way scrounging up photos, ones where she was dressed like the only *known* prostitute in the family. Or maybe, he'd do it the easy way and use her mug-shots. And don't think his name was going in the family and friends section. No, he would leave it at: See Tampa County's Correctional List.

Real rawhide nerve Merda had telling him Mama would want that man's name in her obit. Mama barely knew Parker, and the little she did know, she didn't like.

Things went from bad, straight to Devil's Canyon. Merda escalated from *"why wasn't Parker's name in the obit,"* to… "I don't see why all this time you've been here, you haven't thought about getting a place of your own anyway. For God's sake we all thought you'd be married by now!"

We all!?! Who were we all? No comment. He left out of the house to get some air and clear his head. Bless Mama's heart, her trying to be fair and all, but why she wrote up her Last Will and Testament the way she had, he had no clue. Perhaps she amended the Will when he dropped out of college…when after a year in he realized he couldn't hack it. Maybe that's when Mama got to rewriting the Will, writing in that inane clause he struggled to grasp, '**<u>Contingent upon Clifford staying employed</u>**' *he could remain in the house.*

Or maybe Merda had a hand in changing the Will. That he could believe. She looked changed, but hand to the altar she hadn't changed. Not one micro bit. But if she thought he was going to let her have the only piece of peace he had left, she was in for a tooth and nail fight. He wasn't moving out and that was that. The Will *read*: *'Contingent upon Clifford staying employed'*, in which case he still was.

• • •

That's what Merda didn't know. During all of that time while she was away, piece-milling her soul over to the Lord an arrest warrant at a time, he was home building and polishing his life.

He hadn't caused his parents one iota of trouble, save for the day he dropped out of college. He came right home and by the disappointed look in Mama's eye, but out of the lenient hand his father lent him, steering him to getting that delivery boy position at Linthicum, he buckled down and became a man. Dutifully he went back and forth to work, helped out a great deal around the house, stayed away from trouble, didn't knock up women, and certainly never called *back* home to borrow money from relatives he knew good and well he never was going to repay.

He was the good son who, in their parents ailing years, they relied on. Occasionally Mama would ask if he ever was going to settle down and marry one of the women he introduced the day before he decided *she* wasn't quite right. But Mama didn't make a big deal out of it. Seeing how he renovated the house, going as far as to carve out a room that looked more like an apartment than the bedroom it once used to be, she eased into his lifestyle that intruded on no one.

"Cliff, honey," Mama used to call out to him, "on your way home today would you mind picking up my medicine?" Or, "Cliff, baby, on your way in to work tomorrow, would you mind dropping me off at the hospital? I can catch a cab back."

She knew he wouldn't allow her to catch a fifty-dollar cab ride home. He had moved up the ranks in Linthicum by this time. As an associate he could call in and arrange to take the day off so that he could take Mama to the hospital for her dialysis treatment. Nothing Merda and her selfish self would have stuck her chicken neck out to do.

The kicker was the tone of voice Mama used when she was fed up...usually with Merda. "Cliff, I swear your sister is the work of the devil!"

—so why then hadn't she gotten around to changing her last living testament when for over twenty years, and adding some years for the time Merda spent two-timing and loyally diming-out her *Clyde Burrow* swathe of friends, he spent taking care of them, and working for one employer, Linthicum; and God-willing was soon due to retire.

• • •

The thing was, like the housing market drying up, so were corporations. It wasn't like it was when he started, employees counting down days left until retirement. He had been to dozens of retirement parties, envying those men, and one woman, for serving their time to finally live the other half of their life waking up whenever they felt like it, lounging in front of the television, and taking big fat sloppy vacations at the drop of a hat.

As recent as a few years ago he started counting down the days to his retirement too. Only he didn't count as loudly as the old timers had. This wasn't a day to be making it known he was soon due to retire. Top executives had since turned into leeches, of the thirsty bloodsucking kind, shaving right off the top layers the most senior employees. And they got rid of them for any reason.

Visit the doctor one time too many and it would be, "I'm sorry *sucker*, we need someone who's accountable." Or decline a promotion, which he'd done numerous times, and it might be something like, "I'm sorry *loser*, we need progressive people who take on challenges."

It didn't take long to figure out what was going on. These leeches figured out they could pay four-year graduates four times less than what they were paying old-timers. Everyone was paying into a dried out archaic retirement system that had died years ago. No one was seeing a dime of the money they were, by law, forced to contribute to. Didn't take a second grade mathematician to see the math going on the retirement system.

But Merda wouldn't have understood any of this either. Minimum wage workers and those chronically unemployed, or like the tub she dragged back home and had already found his place slumped in Mama's recliner, knew nothing about what was going on in the work force. They were already retired. All they were waiting on was death.

But then Mama had to die, and Merda return home, and Linthicum to hand him his early walking papers. It didn't happen at once, but it might as well have.

As soon as Merda heard what happened to Mama, she threw a spoon, a fork, a toothbrush, and a lumpy and grumpy Parker into a u-haul and fled like a felon in the night back up to Maryland. Clifford parted the curtains and looked out the window wondering which relative had come to pay their respects by way of a U-haul. The first thing he could think of was which hotel was closet. An affordable one, because this relative was going to need a place to stay that night, and cost was going to be a major concern.

But he caught the peacock head springing out of the cab from the driver's side, and the chiffon scarf, reddish-orange this time, flying behind her. His heart sunk as he watched her mannishly handling Parker, kicking open his wheelchair and hustling around the chair to help him throw a leg at a time out of the cab.

"It stinks in here," was the way she greeted him, as she caught a glimpse of the program he'd been working on. "You haven't found no one to clean this place before people start coming in here..." her voice trailed as she picked up the program, dusting her eyes over the front room, sizing up what she had in mind to claim at the same time.

Up to Mama's final days she kept the house clean. The odor Merda smelled was the lingering lineament scents Mama used to help the swelling in her ankles.

Before he could answer, Merda had breezed up to Mama's room and pried open a safe he had no idea was even in the house. He thought she was going after a typewriter to type up the obituary the way she wanted it written, but instead came rushing downstairs with the Will seized in her hand.

"Alberta and Idell and them will probably be over here in a minute, but I'm telling you right now, ain't nobody *gettin' nothin'*!" And then she asked what were his plans, and when was he moving out.

"Merda, I'm not moving anywhere—"

"—Oh, no Satan…just you wait one red minute! It says right here," the papers squeezed in her grip, "this house belongs to me, and I will be selling it!"

They argued for a minute, before he was able to get her to 'reread' the Will again. That's when he saw the clause, just as he realized the jeopardy he was in.

The day his mother went home, and Merda returned, he was, in fact, the last man of age left at Linthicum; hanging on by a prayer and a wisp of angel hair to a corner office sitting behind a half dozen new graduates. Five more years was all he had left. He didn't have the age to draw on the money, but given his good health and the savings he managed to reinvest, coupled by the trickling of pay he got from freelance writing, in just five more years he'd be able to give Linthicum the thumb and walk out the door a free man. *Good riddance…hope you all live out your time here in misery and in hell!*

But with walking papers in hand and the clause in the Will, he had to walk on eggshells and keep his head down. Wasn't no time to be grand-standing.

So Satan, on this long walk around the block trying to catch a breath of fresh air was going to have to come up with a solid plan.

CHAPTER...2

The plan came out of nowhere? Because honest to goodness he had no plan of action. The idea came out of nowhere. It was Friday and raining, like every other grisly Friday it rained signaling an impending layoff would be hovering between the fog. And this Friday, no different, except raining harder than any Friday he could remember, told him exactly what he was up against.

So why hadn't he called out and stayed home? He could be cozying in his study, adding more keystrokes to his partially finished novel, listening to the pitter-platters pelting his bedroom windows instead watching rain, slamming nails at his brand new Mercury Cruiser, hitting it hard in the face. All this hate. There was no way Linthicum was going to allow him to retire quietly. They'd crunched the numbers, depreciated their assets, and closed their budgets…none too sorry to report, he had to go. He rode out his luck long enough. *Get out you sorry misty-eyed loser*!

Two and a half years, with only two and a half more years to go and this was what it came to. All that time Merda dealt with him locked in the comfort of the shrine he built for himself. He was just about to start his silent celebratory countdown, which the one thing a novelist should be able to handle, and a moonlighting published novelist at that, and that was to come up with a plan. How well he pulled off the plan was another story for another sunshiny day, but coming up with a plot should have been back there lurking in one of his pockets.

But the things he came up with were little more than fleeing thoughts. The old slip and fall was one. He could ride that trip into long-term disability, and from there, right into retirement. There wasn't a day he hadn't thought about trying it. All that held him back were the acting classes he didn't have the nerve to complete. How people could go out on stage in front of full audiences and make those silly dramatic faces, playing out skits that were ridiculous to begin with, embarrassed him.

He thought about it though. He practiced by falling into his study, tripping his foot, sort of like the foxtrot dance where he could even make his shoe come off. But he felt silly doing it. It'd be just his luck that the ruse would be exposed as he stumbled through the slapdash monologue he prepared. It read great on paper, but had him shaking his head when he tried reciting the spill.

As the Mercury inched around the beltway at a dead end snails pace, he pictured the party Merda throwing upon hearing how Linthicum let him go early. It was all in the news, talks of massive layoffs. He hadn't missed that flicker in her eye. There was always that slim chance it would happen to him. And despite her and Parker settling into their new routine there wasn't a day, when she could catch him, her asking how his day had gone. He knew what she was up to, again with that sword behind her back, just waiting on him to trip up and sing her a long song.

Begrudgingly the car slugged onward, him cursing the rain and scoffing about traffic, telling himself that he needed to use the time wisely. Huffing and making the ugly faces at motorists he passed by aiding and abetting in the gridlock; the woman applying eye shadow and the prick reading a newspaper, wasn't going to help ward off Merda if in fact he was getting canned this morning.

Looking at his watch, and then at the clock on the console, his first plan of no action was he didn't want to walk in the office late. Not on this day. If the signs were right, as the burning ulcer in his stomach now indicated, then he wanted to get the news before there were any witnesses. No one could see him walking out of human resources with his head tucked down carrying the last day box with his desk trinkets hanging over the top. As the media figured out, bad news travels fast. And Merda had a host of church friends who loved putting people on the prayer list.

• • •

He got to work to find it gloomier inside. It was so quiet he could hear generators generously pumping heat into the building so that the first arriving employees could have those coffee machines brewing.

But he wasn't a coffee drinker. In fact, he hated that his office was so close to the kitchen. He heard things he'd rather have not heard, how he honed in on picking up signs. One snicker and someone was in there flirting. Two snickers and a whisper, and someone was being set up. Three snickers and if he couldn't log on to the system…it went without mention.

Served him right, perhaps. While everyone was busy partying and screwing over people to get rich quick, just for the hell of it, he was busy working on novels and missing signs of a love to share his life with. He should have married Angelica. Although she was a root canal too sweet and wasn't all that pretty, he was sure Mama would have remembered the Will and rewrote it so that he and Angelica would have a place to stay. But he told Angelica, who was up to calling him five/six times a day, with the sappy-happy sweet sickening voice, to decrease the calls to once a day. She agreed, but didn't tell him she started calling another man the other five/six times a day.

He lost her, but quickly picked up another young woman. She wasn't as sweet, and even less prettier, but she was good company. All he had to do was dial up her number and she would race over to the house like a racehorse, please him for all of ten minutes, and then gallop back out of there. He couldn't remember her name, it was a long time ago, but she was a good one. He pulled off one novel on account her gallop. Made a few grand off the novel too.

After that he saw women here and there, mostly there, until he met Marcella. Now, if there ever was a woman who should have been the one, it would have been Marcella. The woman didn't speak a lick of

English, but seemed to love his novel ideas, yessing anything he said, until Pop's got sick and died. She was Pop's nurse. But he should have gotten that woman's number since they were sleeping together on occasions. The agency who sent her wouldn't release it, and the woman never called the house again.

That was his fault. If only he made it legal because he really liked that woman. If he had gotten down on one knee and asked her to marry him he was positive she may have said yes. At least he thought he was sure. Speaking broken English he wasn't always so certain she understood him. Plus, he wondered what her personal life was like. It sounded like an awful lot of them in one house. Her husband she assured him was out of the picture. She hated the man. He left her for another woman when they arrived in the states. But she kept talking about these sisters and brothers and aunts and uncles and cousins. It sounded like they all lived in the one house with her.

Graciously it was still dark in the office. He dropped his lunch sack on the desk and looked around. There was a chance there was one project left with just enough meat in its budget that an old wishful gaining centurion might have just enough teeth remaining to sink its fangs into. But just in case he might as well look around for something to throw, or maybe punch.

Sitting down at his desk he started to turn on the computer. For reasons unknown, though given all the clearly punctuated signs, he couldn't bring his finger to mash that little circular button. It always took a while for his system to load up, old as it was, but in this case, on this miserable day, he was sure his system would take even longer to load. Like never.

"Clifford, can I speak with you for a minute…ugh, in my office," came a nimble voice crawling over his shoulder, sending one of those chills up his spine. His neck even shirked when he looked around.

Didn't take a faint guess what Shirley wanted. It was Friday, August 28, the date printed in bold on his layoff notice. The one he tried to ignore, like he tried to ignore the rain, and all the women he let slip by, and that praying mantis sister of his.

"Don't bother," he retorted as a surprise to even himself. He hadn't planned to get snappy about the layoff, telling Shirley, "I'll show myself to the door." His plan was to first evade all rainy Fridays, and on Monday go into human resources, and like one other old head had done, beg on his hands and knees for his job. If that didn't work then he was going to see if he could try the skit he'd been halfheartedly rehearsing. Things worked better when they were ad-libbed anyway, like now. He didn't know he was going to snap at Shirley.

Too bad no other employees were in the office. Another skit he played with during one of his desperate dry runs, contemplating the scenario if all crap hit the fan, was going out like a maniac. May as well if his next stop was the streets. Security was always looking for trouble anyways...the same as all of his Armageddon colleagues. During the drag, hopefully by his feet, he was going to recite every bit of gossip he overheard coming out of the kitchen.

*Shirley is a slut! She slept with Paul and the director on the third floor. Kitty is cute, but everyone says she has bad breath. Christina has herpes. They're going to get rid of Pam if she keeps calling out. Bonnie can't spell, a baboon can spell better...*he would say all of this, if Shirley didn't do what had been done with Fred, the only old timer he knew of that wasn't a loser.

Fred went in there and begged to keep his job, except he didn't exactly get down on his hands and knees the way another employee had. He told Shirley he would do anything...and they granted him his wish. His salary was trimmed down and he was flown to a place located in the Pakistan mountains, a position no one had a thing good to say about it because the job always stayed open. Cliff had seen the 'vacant' posting many times. It was the only one open on the board. And now Fred had it, and they hadn't heard from him since.

This was his cue but he didn't take it. He didn't want to be hauled off. And he didn't want the job Fred had taken either, a craftily worded announcement; *'Exciting travel opportunity to train a diverse group of people on projects you'll oversee from implementation to completion.'* In excruciatingly painful small font the location was listed. Looked similar to the location Fred selected, at least it was located in Pakistan, but by the spelling of the city looked a little different. There were more z's and k's in this city's spelling.

Blinded by frustration he hit the elevator call button so forcefully that the covering cracked. He wasn't angry with no one but himself. Individually, to include Merda for the moment, no one had done a thing to him. No one except one. Linthicum. But then Linthicum was nothing but an eleven-story brick building. He was willing to bet if he walked over to any company official, they wouldn't recognize his name from one of Fredrick Douglas's third cousins.

It was too late for planning now. He had to go with the instincts he was born with, which was to quickly exit the building before his photo ended up posted above a CNN headline caption.

He was pulling out of the parking lot before it even registered he lost his job. And as he blew a stop sign he noticed there was one still left! He wasn't the last. There was still a soul survivor. Charlie Willbanks stood almost directly in his path, meekly waving, trying to get him to stop. But his foot was stuck to the accelerator. Charlie jumped back as he breezed on by, perfunctorily aware that if he knocked off a dozen or so baby-boomers in one go at it, it might open up a dozen or so more spots. *Right? Wouldn't it?*

Obviously he wasn't seeing clear. The wild dazed look in Charlie's eye as he shot by told him this. He really wanted to stop and say something to Charlie, something like, "blow up the building!," but then that wouldn't be right either. *Would it?*

He kept going, foot pressed to the metal, zipping out of the garage and over-shooting an island, turning out of the lot on two wheels. He was amazed at how well his new Mercury performed. Car salesmen were the worst lot of scum-sucking crooks, but not Feldman & Sons, the men who sold him the truck. They hadn't shafted him. They swore the baby he drove off the lot would give him one heck of a road performance, and they hadn't lied. Slippery wet roads and that baby hugged tight to the asphalt, spitting at everything it passed.

By the time he got to the first traffic light his foot let go of the pedal some, though the engine continued grinning plenty. Seemed like it was saying, "*more, more,*" egging to show that red light a thing or two, more.

The light turned green and he sat there, debating whether to turn around. *You know you shouldn't have left out like that. What have you been told about burning bridges? And just what are you going to tell Merda?*

Maybe he should have gotten some documentation that he could take to a civilized attorney to prove he had been scammed. *Oh, yeah right Mr. Wronged. Good luck with that sucker!*

In this fusion of murky distress he missed his exit and ended up on Georgia Avenue. It was an exit he missed many times, but those were times when his mind was a less lot foggier. He could see the road ahead and knew which turns would get him back on the beltway. This day he couldn't remember a thing. So he continued on, forgetting how long Georgia Avenue stretched on. A lost motorist could be hours riding out Georgia Avenue.

The rain continued coming down, the wipers going tit-for-tat matching his anxiety. Even the defogger got to huffing, or maybe it was him breathing that hard. He heard the piece of plastic blathering behind him, louder than normal, the result of a crook trying to take from him what didn't belong to them either. He couldn't win for losing, and his losing streak was running like a bow-legged knock-kneed man down a dusty racetrack at an amazing clip. Couldn't this much bad luck be slated for just one person.

He's going down Georgia Avenue, the long stretch that it is, when he sees a quarter-after traffic not more than a fingernail tip away from the passenger door. The woman is large and cloaked in a burqa, double-parked, and hustling children out of a car, one by one, pulling them out by the left arm. *What in the hell was wrong with her*, he was thinking, *leaving those kids wobbling in the street like that*!?! Couldn't she see she was putting them in danger!?! *A deranged man who'd just lost his job was coming up the street!*

He started to blow the horn but in the sequence of events, a man more deranged than him darted out of nowhere and rushed up to his quarter-of side, pressing a deranged look up to his window. "Got a dollar?" the man tried to grin.

It was still happening. He could see it clearly. The bow-legged knock-kneed man had inherited some extra wind and was just turning a corner, though nowhere near to a finish line, yet he was the closet to winning.

He tried to ignore the man. Both of them, the bow-legged knock-kneed one, and the other deranged one still pressed to the window. *The second the light turns green, I'm putting the heat back on the metal*, when with absolutely no warning in sight, the deranged man goes behind his back and whips out an instrument of what looked like could cause mass destruction, and flipped on the hood of the car. It happened in a maddening hazy flash. All he saw were two feet go up in the air and this weapon of mass destruction suddenly appear.

In that split second, unsure of what the deranged stranger held in his hand, he would have sworn to any dieter that it was possible to shed fifty-pounds in less than a second.

He only realized it wasn't a pipe or a sub-machine gun when the man began fiercely wiping the window, smearing grime and grease across the front windshield with what turned out to be a dry squeezy.

Cliff tapped the horn and hissed, "get off the car! Get off the car!," and wanted to call the man a mean name for good measure but was afraid he might have to live up to those words. So he kept tapping the window, and the gas pedal, waving and hissing, trying to get the man's attention.

The man stayed there, no bucket, so no water, but wielding a squeezy he kept busy attending to smearing filmy dirt across the windshield. Horns blared behind him. But no one but him could see the mad man on the hood until they sped around him. Some still flipped him the bird, having no sympathy for him, or the man slipping and sliding over the hood. *This couldn't be real.*

In the many years he worked at Linthicum he heard a small collection of happenings witnessed by colleagues on this stretch of road, but nothing like this. The worst he remembered was the account of where one woman stuck her arm in a car and grabbed a bagel out of the driver's hand. She ate the bagel on the spot, right in front of the bedizened man.

Clifford continued alternating between tapping the break and gas, trying to get the man off the car. "Get off the car! Move! Get off!" But the man hung on.

Desperately looking around, hoping one of the horn blowers piling up behind might have mercy on him, or at least the other deranged man, but no such hope was in sight. Like the woman in the burqa, this man too could have been pretty badly hurt. All he had to do was show everyone what *his baby* could do. *Who could live with something like that on their conscience?* Apparently many. Every one of them laid on those horns as if they wanted to see blood shed first.

Was humankind reverting back into itself? Returning to the barbaric behaviors they had built technologies to escape? A young woman who swerved around him, face contorted as nothing even Ifukube could create, passed him the finger, and had she bothered to roll the window down, she probably could have passed him Godzilla's breath too. *What had gotten into people?* Not only the derelict still strapped to the hood of the car, but on down to include the leeches who let him go.

Finding his own wits end he reached into the ashtray and grabbed a fist full of coins. Working with both hands he quickly he threw the gear in park while rolling the window down in a maneuver that belonged in Baileys and Barnum Circus. Hard, as hard as he could, he threw the coins over the hood of the car. A quarter must have hit the man because he grabbed one eye, rolling over the hood, playing both parts of cops and robbers. It was one hell of a class-act, the class-act he wanted to give Linthicum…and Shirley, but didn't have the nerve to do.

Laid flat on his back the man started kicking and screaming, "You got me! You got me! I'm out! I'm out!" It was an immobilizing class-act. One that made his throat swell and his heart jumped down to his socks. What was the man going to do when he ran out of act? Punch through the window and snatch him out of the car? Sue him? Or finish smearing his windows and demand his just compensation? The dollar he asked for to begin with.

On the dime the man stopped screaming, opened one eye to asses his damage when he realized what was in his hand, the thing that hit him. *Money*! It looked like he was thinking. *It's raining money*!

The man popped right up and in a wild sweep he swept over the hood of the car, scooping up as many coins as he could. It was another five-minute Hall of Fame Broadway act watching the man on his hands and knees searching the hood for more coins.

The street light must have changed a hundred times. Cliff imagined a skycam reporting the cause of the traffic jam on Georgia Avenue; a silver car, unknown make and model, "blocking traffic!" Forget mentioning the deranged man running circles in front of his car still searching for coins. It would all be his fault as the bow-legged knock-kneed man continued around the track closing in for the win.

Crazed and dazed, but elated, the man rushed over to his window. "Thank you sir. Thank you." And just like he appeared out of nowhere, he dismantled into nowhere, scurrying across the street in a limping fashion to blend in with the fog. The only evidence of his presence he left lying on the hood of the car.

Unnerved Cliff got out of the car and grabbed the squeezy, laying it on the seat beside him. *What the devil*, and then a horn bellowed behind him.

• • •

Although he had to sequester the delirium of the bow-legged knock-kneed man still running his race around a dusty racetrack, following the signs he'd come to rely on was about as to near to anything spiritual that resembled religion. The deranged man and his squeezy was a sign, though telling him what, he didn't know.

Instinctively he picked Merda to blame. If it hadn't been for her, none of this would mean anything. He probably could've even worked his own skit on Shirley had not he been so hung up on the thought of losing his job, and then home, all in one domino shot. Like always it was Merda's fault, and he wasn't thinking this in a self-pitying way. It really was her fault. Like she wooed gullible people with that cooing voice of hers, she could have fished out some cooing wisdom and compassion and seen it wasn't the spiritual thing to do, threatening to throw him out in the street.

Come on…the woman went to church, religiously, every Sunday. He overheard her bragging on the phone about all the missionary work she was involved with. Mondays and Tuesdays she worked at the children's home, cradling homeless children with her love. *Huh?* Wednesdays she volunteered at the battered women's shelter, showering homeless women with her support. *Huh? Huh?* Thursdays she was down at the soup kitchen ten hours a day, feeding homeless families meals. *Huh? Huh? Huh?* Did homelessness mean anything? Or was it her mission to add to the homeless audience so that she'd have something else to brag about?

At sixty-five and pushing it, Merda still was a good-looking woman. Cough, cough. He heard her bragging about this too. Behind Parker's back however. So her legs were a little long and not in the best of shape, but it did make her look taller. And so her complexion was a little blotchy and wrinkly around her eyes and lips, but at least the light patches allowed people to refer to her as a redbone. All she had to do, which she did, was jazz up the tinseling of copper hair on her head by moussing it into cute little curls and garnishing her leftovers with fake lashes, nails, and enough jewelry to open another Zales. And oh, add on the cooing mooing voice and everyone saw her as a mesmeric rejuvenated savior.

The truth was, the way he saw her, Merda's heart was little more than a bawled up knot. And how he knew this was by simple things such as how she handled her infertility issue. Instead of trying to adopt a child, which he thanked every angel she worshipped she didn't try, she settled the matter of being unable to bear children by adopting dogs.

The first dog she got was a Beagle. Someone found him on a highway, emaciated and fearful. But ten days later the dog, still a little emaciated, and probably even more alarmed, took off again.

He suggested getting a small dog, one she could maintain easier, given the hours she and fatso did nothing around the house, but no, she was set on the larger dogs. She claimed their temperament was better.

Well, along comes Mr. Chef, a big gruffy looking Saint Bernard, and fat ass Harriet, a boxer. Forget the fact that the dogs didn't get along and tore up the house after left alone for under an hour, but they almost tore Merda apart when she tried to separate them. They had Mr. Chef and Harriet all of 17-hours before Merda was on her way back to the rescue center.

Mr. Bean was the best. He was a mutt, some mix of terrier so lonely that the connection was instantaneous. But Merda saw that, him and Mr. Bean getting along, and right back to the pound he went too. A day after Mr. Bean she came back with another double wham slam.

She brought home Dutchie, a Dogo, and Echo, an Eskimo. That's when he got another sign. She was trying to kill him. Both dogs hated him, and that was from the first day he met them. Echo, nine months and Dutchie, two, tore after him the moment he stepped foot out of the car. It was a good thing they made their displeasure known immediately. He could have been one step in the door and ended up in several thousand pieces. Head in three states and torso spread across the world. *Hello, it's Cliff down here. I know it's a partial toe, but this partial toe belongs in Maryland.* He was convinced Merda planned the attack, angsty about him not leaving.

On the beltway, the rain continued coming down at a steady maddening pace, forcing the wipers to work twice as hard. For every cloud in the sky, there was supposed to be a silver-lining, a favorite phrase of his mother's. But just where, at the moment he couldn't tell. If there were any silver-linings up there, he must have been calling them lightening. A favorite catch phrase of his, also pawned by his mother was, "two's company, three's a crowd." Fired or not, he didn't care. Merda and fatso could pack up and go because he wasn't moving anywhere!

CHAPTER...3

Barnes and Noble, book haven of America, that's where he ended up on that cheerless day. Tacoma Park, a few exits before the exit that would take him home was where he found himself loafing away half a day. He couldn't face Merda broken and spineless. He needed an escarpment of coffee, sugar, and cream to rasterize his thoughts and help him think of a way to get Merda off his back, and maybe even, the fatso out of Mama's chair.

His mother couldn't have wanted this. His father certainly wouldn't have wanted this. He never approved of the way Merda led her life, and approved even less of

Parker. When he heard Merda had cleaned up her act and met a really *nice young boy*, he grunted and looked the other way, refusing to talk about what he thought of her so-called improvement. And when he heard she was marrying the really *nice young boy*, and everyone got to making plans for that big trip to Florida, he claimed he lost his nerve for flying, despite his flying all the time, and never mind the fact that they all drove to Florida.

Cliff sat in the balcony of Barnes and Noble, in a far back corner with a pound of books sitting in his lap and a judicious selection of warm colors coalescing around him, pouring over his next steps. He didn't think he'd find an answer in one of the books lying in his lap, but just the same picked up one to thumb through.

The home-keeping book he flipped through first. He always liked Martha Stewart. He thought she'd gotten the shaft too. So it was a little tough seeing her with a roll of paper towels in hand, and smiling. *How could anyone have that big of a smile on their face after being shafted like that*? He dropped the book on the floor, moving to the next. The hallow look in her eyes bothered him, too.

The parachute book he got rid of too. But *Shit My Dad Says* hit him in the gut. Reading and laughing, he had almost reached the center of the book when he realized almost an hour had gone by. He expected that golden gem to be going to the counter with him.

Thumbing through the other books cradled in his lap he went back to the parachute book lying on the floor. The *What Color is Your Parachute*? He didn't get past the first page before his mouth felt parched and his throat started burning. He tried to look down at the book again but this time the sheet turned white and he couldn't see a thing. He swallowed, and swallowed hard. He felt like hurting the book, which for the moment the best way to achieve that goal was by slapping Patterson's book on top of it. '*Sonofagun probably wasn't even ten!*'

Before he knew it, he was standing before a small girl staring across a counter at him. She must have asked if she could help him because it dawn on him that she was waiting on his answer.

'*Miss, can you please call a manager over here…to come and kill a book?*' That's what he felt like saying, but didn't. Instead he did the sensible thing and squinted, trying to read the drink of the day's price list.

"I think I'll have…" and he thought back a moment, digging in pants pockets, scrounging around for change but only feeling lint. He must have thrown six or seven dollars at the squeezy window-washing guy. There were a ton of quarters in the astray, but damn it if there was a dime in any one of his pockets.

He pictured the derelict, probably at a chicken shack, gumming down a delicious chicken sandwich on his last quarters, and here he couldn't scrounge up a dime to pay for a hot cup of water.

"Never mind," and he laid the thumbed through *shit* book on the counter and left the store.

It was a good laugh that failed. He didn't get to smile until he looked to his left and saw the Dress Barn, where he could *dress for less*. How all of this fused into one heroic idea was a wonderment all to its own. But there it was; the *dress for less* Barn, the panhandling derelict, tax-free money, the shit book, Linthicum, Merda, and the suited up hunger and thirst for revenge.

He smiled gallantly. Merda talked a lot about divine intervention, and man-o-man was he not now lapping up in the thrill of it. This would be a throw back at life, slapping in the face everyone and anything that ever dared to pin him to the underclass. All of his life he tried doing the right thing, keeping his head down and his emotions rolled down to the edge of his sleeves. Now it was time to get even shafting all the villains who shafted him. For once, he was breaking the rules. Satan was pulling on boxing gloves and going out *dressing for less.*

Full of bitter hope, he walked into the Dress Barn welcomed by a bright spray of lights and a friendly young girl grinning his way.

"Hello, welcome to Dress Barn," she greeted him with a clipboard pressed against her small chest and a warm smile careening across her face. "Let me know if I can be of assistance," she hummed as she turned to hum the same tune to a woman coming in behind him.

He pulled her by the arm, interrupting her work. The woman behind him didn't look to need help. He was the one who needed help. Merda, as shamed as he was to admit it, so sssh...but he had never gone shopping for clothes for himself. Yeah, on occasion he picked up a jacket here and socks and maybe briefs here and there, but full fledge shopping for clothes was something he never did. Just so happened, his father was one of the best dressers in the world. He closeted suits like no one's business. And since they wore the same size, his closet full of suits he inherited. And what he didn't inherit he received as gifts. Mama bought him tons of shirts, and yes, Merda had bought him a few things too.

"Cliff," she asked one day, a month after moving in, "is that Dad's sweater?"

He had to look at what he was wearing. He got lots of compliments on the styles he fashioned. It happened to be how he moved up the ranks at Linthicum. Highly unlikely, but maybe she, too, was going to compliment him. "Yes, it is," he answered hesitantly, rethinking where she was going with the question. Perhaps not only did she want him out of the house, but also wanted the clothes on his back.

"Cliff, how are you going to meet someone dressed in Dad's old clothes? That sweater has to be old as me. I remember Dad wearing it when he used to walk me to school!"

Indeed that was a long time ago and indeed the sweater was that old. But look at who was talking. She thought she still had it. The next night she came home carrying a large environmental friendly Big Brown shopping bag. Inside were a few hoodies, and denims, and a leather jacket—the Fonzie kind. *Was this the new look*? He wasn't sure. None of it was his style. He was more of a khaki-sweater type guy, when he wasn't suited up in one of his father's light-weight worsted wool suits, no more than three buttons. But then Merda had always kept up with fashion, on the opposite side of the aisle however. The type men she crooned over were the type men he avoided. He certainly wasn't up for mimicking any parts of their style.

Yet, they were good clothes, the quality that being. It added to his wardrobe, another reason why he didn't shop for himself.

"I'm looking for work clothes. Do you know where I can find them?" he asked the upbeat sales woman.

"Sure sir," and in this upbeat fashion she pointed to the far back of the store. "Over there in that corner is where you'll find men's wear."

He squinted, looking in the direction of where she pointed. "Ugh, but..." and he stuttered, "...ugh, I think I'm going to need a little help picking out what I need." For this gig he would need advice. Surely beggars didn't shop for themselves either. They wore what was handed to them out of Goodwill, *didn't they*?

The young woman drew back. He didn't realize he'd latched onto her arm. He looked down and found he was clutching her pretty tightly. "Oh, I'm sorry," and he let go. "It's just that I'm not sure what sizes to get."

Curiously, slowly looking him over, as if he'd come out of the cave ages, she led him to the men's section. "Do you prefer Dockers or denims?"

He took a wild guess. "...Ugh, I think I'll go with the denims," he answered, rounding up the excitement.

"...But they can't look new," he thoughtfully threw in. He couldn't tell the woman exactly what he was up to, but throwing out little hints like this would get him a lot closer to the look he was aiming for rather than him trying to pick out the clothes, or worse, Merda.

Again, the young woman curiously inspected him. "Well, there are a few pre-washed jeans in here." She looked down at him again, "what size do you normally wear?"

"I'm not sure." He stammered, "...ugh, see the thing is, my (*muttering*) buys all of my pants."

"Ah ha," the woman gladly expelled, satisfied with the explanation. It explained the oddness. "You look like a 33," and she pulled a pair of size-33 pre-washed denims from a rack and handed them to him.

"I'll need a shirt too," he said standing there as if he needed help getting dressed too. "One not too flashy, something plain," he remembered to add.

"Flannel maybe?" She sarcastically asked, though he didn't catch her drift.

"Yeah, sure," he shrugged. Flannel sounded warm enough for the season. He had a pair of flannel pajamas and loved wearing them when it got cold out.

She grabbed a cotton shirt sliding off a hanger and pressed it against him. "Looks like it'll fit," she smiled.

"Yes, I'm sure it will," he greedily grinned, leaning into her eyes as if he wanted to fall in.

"The dressing room is over there," she pointed behind him, stacking the shirt on top of the small pile of clothes cradled in his arms.

"Oh, I'm going to need some beat up running shoes too," he said looming above the pile.

Now the woman was back to looking concerned. Was he planning on holding up the store after he got all of these clothes… with her help!?!

"Sir, the shoes are over there," firmly pointing to a shoe rack a short distance away. "If you need any other assistance, just ask the salesperson over there," and she briskly walked away.

Clutching the flannel shirt and denims crammed in his arms, he rushed over to the shoe area. He wasn't in a hurry, but the excitement added to his hastened steps. Scurrying up and down the shoe aisle, he ran his eyes up and down the wall of shoes. It was women's aisle but he didn't know the difference. He skipped over the heels, assuming the men's and women's shoes were mixed in, and concentrated on finding something black, and a size too small. It would build credibility. Make him look like the real deal...like a true societal reject.

At the register, watching the screen tallying his total, he calculated his earnings. All he needed to do was hustle a dollar out of 500 people a day, only five days a week. That left Saturday and Sunday open. He'd be his own boss. Could call out when he wanted. And at ten grand a month, he could fully retire in five months. No, he wasn't hurting for money. It would be just enough tax-free money to get back at everyone on his get-back list. Even if he got five grand, it would be enough to satisfy his curiosity. He opened his eyes to see the cashier giving him that look the greeter gave him when he approached her.

"That's $69.72," the cashier said in a leery voice, as if waiting on the moment when it was time to scream.

"Wow, rags sure are expensive," he gaily chuckled, fishing in his back pocket and pulling out a credit card.

"Just slide the card in the reader," the clerk tersely instructed, still wearing the leery look, and Ragamuffin keep moving body language.

But did he notice, or even care? No, he caught none of the attitude, He snatched the receipt, grabbed his bag and gleamed wildly in an upbeat stroll out of the store. The rain had stopped and a plucky sky opened up the vision of setting the world on fire. Satan Blanchard was stepping up to the batter's plate and taking a swing.

• • •

The melancholy came back the moment he walked into the house. There sat Parker, swelled up and bubbling as if any day he might walk in and find him spilling over his mother's lounge chair. The TV was on, the sole source of light in the front room, and Parker was pointed in that direction. He walked by him without greeting him. This was the norm. They rarely spoke. Unless they happened to be watching a game together, usually around holidays when family and friends were over, did they expend the extra energy to share what little they had in common. He just couldn't appreciate a man that didn't leave the house to make an earning.

Any moment Merda would be home, nosing around in his business, always with the usual fabricated motive, *when was he leaving*? It was Friday, so this was the day she spent in the church, *tallying donations* so she claimed. It was hard to believe Pastor Edmonds had that much trust in her. For God's sake, why he refused to believe the woman was a career thief, it was a vague secret. He just couldn't buy that business of *lost but found*, and saved by the grace of His good mercy. Someone like her counting his money, he'd have to tell to guess what was in the safe. If she guessed correctly, or almost correctly ten times in a row, then he'd let her volunteer her services as a fortune-teller…somewhere other than in his church.

Like everyday since they had been there, he went to his room and locked the door behind him. Before they came home he used to leave the door open, but now he kept the room secured by a fairly decent Magnum 365 deadbolt. Yeah, she was sweet as pie, and saved, but the deadbolt summed up how much faith he had in her comeback. The seclusion was a nice way to put distance between them and keep the arguing at a safe level. He also didn't have to see her everyday. Parker, there wasn't much choice, since the man went nowhere, except from the frig to the chair, and maybe to the toilet. Sometimes he smelled so bad, he doubted if he did that.

Staying in the room kept him away from all of that and allowed him to write more. His latest novel, *Satan's Best Friend*, a screwball tale about the devil and an evil goddess, had picked up quite a bit of steam. Fine-combing through the completed draft he found the main characters finally coming to life. Parker was Exodus in the story. Merda the evil goddess of course. And he got the starring role—Satan.

Merda's return home made it an easy rewrite. Before he couldn't stay motivated to keep the story going. He couldn't visualize the characters, trying to create them from a collage of mythology novels he read—namely *Gates of Fire*. Latching on to the Greek names grew to be a pain and getting the characters beyond seeing evil became a chore. But the idea of avenging aristocrats stayed wide-awake. And when Merda and the waffle traipsed into town, he opened up the document and almost in one night rewrote a second draft.

Patalonia he was calling her. He liked the Greek ring to the name, and the fact that under this guise he could expose her secrets in complete obscurity. This would spare him of reliving the real reason he hated her thumping the Bible, while ripping her to shreds.

The tale opened on a day if he lived to be a million he'd never forget. The day he out sung the choirmaster and forever left the church and never looked back. It was a Sunday, and Pearl, a heavy-set woman who sang like Mahalia, just louder, was singing. Pearl had one of them wide-open mouths that even when her mouth was shut, which it rarely was, a line stretched clear from one side of her face to the other. And she always outlined her lips in every color of the rainbow too, to make the line longer, and sometimes wider. But more notable than all of this was her operatic deep voice she, and many others, were so happy with. No one in the history of church ever dared to cross Pearl by out singing her.

...All except for this one tepid Sunday. It happened at Cedar Baptist Church at the 11am service. It was an old small church where the little ones, on up to the choirmaster, all sang together. Usually everyone backed up the lead singer, which more often than not was Pearl, who she sang the solo with them holding up the rear singing the repeat verses.

But this Sunday they were singing *Troubles of the World* and *Precious Lord* by Mahalia Jackson, his favorite gospel songstress, and *Jesus is My Rock*, another one of his favorites. He had his mother dress him in his best suit too. A little tailored pinstripe suit his father had tailored for Easter. He wore the hat, gloves, and shiny patent leather shoes with it.

They came down the aisles that day, as they did every Sunday, all of them swinging the two-step bump to the instrumentals of *Jesus is My Rock,* prepping the church for what was to come. With his favorite songs all lined up, this was going to be the Sunday they would take the church to heaven.

When they got up on the altar to the pews where the choir sang from, the church was happy. Eyes closed, hands swaying, and rocking in a motion that made the floorboards and walls hum, the church was ready to be delivered… and he, on this special Sunday wanted to be the one soul to deliver them.

Even before he did, he planned to put all of his heart into the songs sang that day. They started out with *Troubles of the World* and it went on from there. This was the solo they were to back up Pearl cooing to the instrumentals, except he couldn't hold it any longer. He could see some worshippers already crying, but they weren't crying hard enough. So he stepped in, with his small but mighty voice, drawing on verses Pearl wasn't carrying home the way the people, and he, wanted her to. He could feel it.

Mouths fell open and people stood when he came out of the pew with his large little voice. At first shaking their heads and then spilling in the aisle clapping their hands, and crying a stream of tears filled him even more. So he got deeper, the way his father sounded in the shower, even bending over his little ten-year old body to pull up them notes with all of his strength, from the diaphragm like Pearl taught them. It took a while for the church to settle and wasn't long before he was back at it again. The very next song in fact, *Jesus is My Rock*, he took the church home again. Generously but innocently his voice jutted ahead of everyone, carrying on out of the church doors. The effulgent hearty sound sent people leaping to their feet. The congregation swayed and cried. Some sang with him. Others rejoiced in the aisles shouting, dancing, passing out…the church rocked.

He never saw Pearl's expression, but by the way the church responded he assumed she was hanging in there with him. He thought he had done a good job, what God had guided him to do. It was only after service, on the way walking home with Merda yanking him and hitting him in the back of the head when he realized he had committed the ultimate sin. He out sung Pearl.

His parents weren't home. Back then they used to spend Sunday mornings with their father's mother, so it was Merda who gave him a beating he would never forget. She beat him so bad he developed a fever. After that he never went to church or sung again.

That's exactly how he opened chapter one, except for meticulously veiling every word he could with its Greek replacement. No one would know he was writing about a 16th century spiritually grounded motherless whore.

This was the best way to kill off the spirit that killed his spirit. He didn't have to wait on an apology or argue with her or address the matter in any other manner. What was done, was done. If she really wanted to be a better person, she would have been a better person. And if she could be forgiven, then surely he'd be forgiven for writing literature that only he knew the subtext.

• • •

He emptied his briefcase, dumping the apathetic papers that belonged to Linthicum in the wastebasket. Many were marked confidential, and some (by law) he was required to return. Too bad. They should have secured their assets when they first thought about giving him the shaft. He didn't even bother shredding them. Pay stubs, insurance papers, bills, and scratch pieces of paper with notes for future material all went in the wastebasket.

He stared into his closet, a room about the size of a small bedroom, surveying the wall of suits his father left behind. Like his father used to do, he kept the suits arranged by color. He watched ivory slither to black. He might as well get rid of them too. He had no use for them. This was it. He'd long ago given up on church, and now he was officially retired. He started filling a trash bag with the suits. No one was into vintage clothes. Not even for Halloween. But there were a lot of suits, and remembering the time, it wouldn't be long before Merda would be home. He'd better run the trash out before she got in, if he wanted to avoid her pestering and be good and locked in his sanctuary before she got home. He could rub her face *in it* later.

Passing by Parker, looking more like a statue than a human, with that remote sitting in his lap, a remote he vowed never to touch, he carried the large brown plastic bags out back. A normal person may have asked if he needed help, or looked interested. He could be asked to describe what he saw, but wouldn't have a clue. And then again, that was okay too. Of all people he needed to be locked up. Even if it was for sitting in his mother's lounge chair perpetrating a fraud.

Cliff hurled the trash bags in the outside dumpster and poured ammonia on top. Merda didn't like him doing this. She said it was cruelty to the animals that liked to gnaw their way into the plastic canister and eat the garbage. For that reason he poured half the bottle on top of the trash. The smell wouldn't let him peek too long, but what he could see from partial eyesight, his deed was well covered. He made it back to his room just as Merda hustled in the house.

"Cliff! Cliff!" and she shouted, turning to Parker staring transfixed into the tube, "have you seen Cliff?"

"Ugh…he just went in *that* room."

"Cliff! Cliff!" banging with both fists on his door. "Cliff, you in there?"

What the heck, at least he hadn't yet turned on the PC. He unlocked and opened the door slightly. "I just got in. You need something?"

"No, I was just wondering how you got home so fast. The beltway was a parking lot when I got on."

It would have been for him too, except he wasn't on the beltway at his usual time. He was sitting comfortably in Barnes and Noble. "Oh, I had a headache," he answered wearily. "I left early today," the best excuse in the world. It gave him two reasons to close his door without letting her further the investigation.

"You should take one of those roots in the frig with some of that chai tea. Do you want me to make you a cup," she asked headed back to kitchen, where she spent the other half of her day.

Hell No! Though he didn't say this. Well, he didn't say it like this. "No, that's okay," was how he put it. After he closed the door he added, "I'll poison my own self, thank you very much!"

"I'll put on some water," she answered anyway, not hearing him. "I think I'm going to get a little myself," she sighed, squinting when she happened to catch a glimpse of what was going on outside.

"Cliff!" and she yelled out as if Parker was attacking her. It was one of those long drawn out echoing Cliffs. Sounded like her last words before falling off a cliff.

He hurriedly unlocked the door and rushed into the kitchen to join her at the window. Parker hadn't moved a muscle. It didn't even look like he leaned forward, curious none about the screaming. Right away Cliff saw the problem, and understood Parker's lack of concern. Dutchie and Echo had gotten a hold of the trashcan. They had strewn trash across the yard. And who else but him ever took out the trash?

"Don't worry, I'll take care of it," though she wasn't half as worried as him. Dutchie was lying on one of his father's jackets. Laying on it like he owned it, and planned to wear it one day.

The moment he stepped out of the back door, the pups were up on their feet, ears at full attention ready to pounce. Echo stood first. He was Merda's favorite. And his least favorite. Like the hateful pup-mate he was, he came at him baring his teeth and snarling. Not sure if Merda was watching from the window, and fearing taking his eyes off Echo and turning around, he felt his pockets for keys. He kept a tazer on the ring.

"Take another step you dumb mutt and I'll taze your butt to hell." Dogs understood language better than most people gave them credit for. Echo didn't move. But not moving wasn't all of a good thing. He needed to get the clothes back in the trashcan, and he needed to do this fairly quickly. Having to keep his eyes trained on Echo wasn't a good thing.

He tried to ignore him, reaching for a pair of pants he saw out the corner of one eye when the fifty-pound pup lunged at him, forcing him to fall backwards. As both feet flew up in the air he saw a flash of himself starring in the movie Cujo. Echo came at him, as if he was coming out of the sky, looking like a devil with wings and canine fangs.

"Get back! Get off of me you dumb mutt," and he rolled over, James Bond style, squeezing on the tazer as he rolled. Miraculously, somehow, he managed to get Echo in the eye. Echo squealed once and backed away, taking off in this spastic run to other side of the yard. It looked like he was running in circles, going mad it seemed, but he couldn't be sure because as he was rising up from his knees he caught Dutchie getting up off the jacket and sprinting his way…fast.

There wasn't any barking, at least not coming from Dutchie, perhaps she didn't have enough time to bark being in a brisk haste to tear a hole in his backside. In the scuffle with Echo he lost the tazer, but gained a handful of grass and one trashcan lid, what he used to sock Dutchie in the head with.

Merda rushed out into the yard, bursting through the backdoor as if she was coming to his defense, though he knew it was the other way around.

"What's going on out here? What happened? "Did you forget to tie down the lid?" she accusatorily beleaguered. Now, was that anything to ask when their 70-pound pup was standing there snarling at him.

Oh course he forgot to tie the lid down. How else had the yard gotten trashed. *Damn dogs*! But he said none of this. He only winced about the small puncture Echo managed to put in his leg.

"Go put some peroxide on that," Merda ordered, ignoring his torn trousers and the suits still strewn over the yard. She ran off to comfort Echo, Dutchie following her being the smart heifer she was. Surely she wasn't coming back for more, not with Echo going off like a siren behind him, throwing himself into the fence.

• • •

Just like Merda she thought he should pay for the expensive emergency room dog doctor visit. Fifteen hundred bucks that visit cost. Turned out something got Echo in the eye. She wanted to know if he hit Echo with something, which he claimed he didn't know. What he knew for sure was he was in a fight for his life.

"Well Cliff, you've got to help me take care of this. I don't have fifteen hundred dollars lying around."

And neither did he. Plus, they were her dogs. They had no business attacking him. But as usual, he said none of this. He acted like he hadn't been just let go and wrote out a check for half the cost of the doctor's visit.

"And I'm going to need help paying for his meds too. Whatever it was you hit him with, it burned his eyes!" And she said it as if it was all his fault.

But he paid for the meds too. Just don't ask him to take care of his eye. Not if she wants the damn dog to have any eyes.

For once in his life, other than writing novels, he was just happy to have a plan. A pretty convincing plan so he thought. He had written it all out, separated by chapters, guaranteed to be a best seller after *Satan's Best Friend*. When those puppies hit the market, they'd either love it, or hate it, but *everybody* was going to read it.

The plan was to leave the same time, dressed in one of the two suits he had left, and drive the same route he'd driven to Linthicum for the past twenty-two years. Instead of pulling onto Linthicum's parking lot however, he would find a public restroom and change into his *Dress for Less*. That's what he did the following morning.

He woke up, before Merda, showered, shaved, and grabbed a cup of coffee before hopping into the truck.

The moment he got in the truck he realized one small hiccup. Somehow he had to figure out a way to forgo the shaving. Merda surely would notice if he missed shaving. Maybe he could come up with an excuse, like telling her *they* moved him to a new department, undercover work that she couldn't nose into. That was a good one. One thought he thought to keep in his back pocket. She always read those mystery books. She'd have to love believing that lie.

The Sheraton's parking lot was full when he arrived, so he parked on the street. It was a three-hour meter he parked beside, which concerned him at first. It wasn't quite 7:30(am). That meant he'd have to slug it back over to the meter at least three times. But then he shrugged it off since he'd be wandering around anyway. He just had to remember to keep track of the check-in times; 10:30, 1:30, and 4:30.

The Sheraton brimmed with activity. This was where he planned to change. Didn't think he was going to start out in a coffee shop public restroom? This gig required that he glide into it, not jump in head first. He wanted comfort, and the Sheraton with its brilliant lights, marble and wood fixtures, and bellhops hurrying by carrying important peoples necessaries provided that. Of course too, this would be the time that someone would spot and recognize him. Despite being to hundreds of these conferences before, no one ever could place his face, snapping their fingers and holding their chins trying to remember when they met. *Hey Joe! You only pass me everyday on your way to your office. I sit in the corner office you tart*! Yeah, just when he didn't need the visibility, he'd get it. They wouldn't recall a thing about the conference other than seeing him, visibly dressed like a vagabond. "*Did anyone see Cliff? Is Cliff okay? I saw him at the Sheraton. He looked down on his luck.*"

Without making eye contact, he slinked his way into a restroom and into a stall. *Man*, he muttered, struggling to pull on the pants. *He should have tried them on*. He couldn't tell if it was the stall or the pants that was too small. Only after he managed to get the pants on did he realize it probably were the pants. Gathered around his crotch and snatched up his butt the way they were, he decided not to tuck in the shirt. But the shirt was just as bad, almost reaching his knees.

He emerged from the stall a little sweaty, and looked in the mirror. Awful. That's how he looked. Plain awful. And not in a good nomadic way. He looked awful in a way that a derelict might call him a farmer, and a farmer might call him a refugee. A huge question mark and a small semi colon was what he saw facing him.

Making his way back into lobby, steering through the throng of people, he wasn't the only one espying his questionable look. A security guard spotted him and stopped him right away.

"Excuse me," and the guard stepped in front of him, blocking his way. "Where are you going with that?"

Stumped, not to mention crazed with fear hoping no one caught the exchange, he searched himself for an answer. "With what?"

"With that," the guard repeated, nodding towards the briefcase.

"Oh this," and he relaxed, dropping his arms and sheepishly grinning. "This is my briefcase," he tried to laugh off, expecting to soon be on his way.

The guard muttered something into his shoulder and then abruptly grabbed him beneath the arm, strong-holding him, leading him into a hidden *back* office.

Who was this fifty-cent security guard with the lava mocha dark lips wearing a jacket that looked like it was hanging on a gorilla's coat hanger? He started to protest until he looked around. Several pairs of eyes curiously inspected him, staring him up and down as if at any moment one of them would knock on his head and ask if he was inside. *Come on Cliff, we know it's you. You can't hide in there. We see you.* Before erupting into a laugh so hideous he'd have to laugh too, and admit it was him.

Humbly, with his briefcase tucked securely beneath his arm he faced a room full of law people, some with guns upholstered to their hips, others dressed in white short sleeve shirts with coffee stains resting in odd places beneath their chins. *Things would get sorted out and fixed once he was able to explain his side of the story*, he smartly expected would happen.

At first no one spoke, not even to *lava lips the big gorilla*, pompously pacing around as if he'd caught a great big *black* shark. Moving in a manner that assumed his guilt...pouring more coffee, tossing a pencil to the next guy over, and answering calls with, "yeah?," they ignored him as if he didn't have some place to be. He could end up with three tickets and two boots on his car by the time he got out of there.

"Hey, look guys," he volunteered. "I really need to be getting to work." It was an ingenious spill, one that slipped out of desperation, visualizing two booted tires and the story he would have to trump up for Merda.

The short seriously round mushy guy looked up. "Work," he asked as if the term was foreign to him.

"Yes, I'm working undercover...and you guys are seriously about to blow it." He wanted to call them nimrods too, but left that part out.

"Do you have some ID," the seriously round guy asked in a tone that measured sudden concern.

He reached in his back pocket and pulled out his wallet. Driver's License, credit cards, medical cards, he pulled all the cards out of his wallet and spread them before a suddenly wide-awake small hotel security force.

The seriously round guy wheeled around in his chair to take a good hard look at *lava lips*. He threw up his hands like a wasted effort. "So what do you have on him," he asked from a tiresome bothered voice.

"Ugh, we just saw the guy walking around with that briefcase beneath his arm," *lava lips the gorilla* mumbled. He was getting chewed out after this was over. That much was for certain.

The round fella sighed loudly and shook his head, tossing the wallet across the desk. Disgusted, he waved Cliff away. "Go on and get out of here," he fanned towards the door.

An explosion of laughter followed him on out the door. "Damn, wonder what they're paying him?"

"Must be one hell of a combat pay…"

"Got him sticking out like candlelights," the chuckles retorted, chasing him into a frazzled chaotic lobby more disorienting than the chuckles hounding behind him.

CHAPTER...4

Note to himself. No more Clifford. That man was gone, his name stricken from his vocabulary. It wasn't a part of the plan, a step he missed. He had to insert that part of the plan in. He was now Norman. Why he chose Norman, he had no idea. The name just caught him by the ear, likely klept from the *Cheers* character. He openly identified with a man wasting away on a barstool, staring down at his life swimming in the bottom of a beer mug, an iodine reflection of pity he couldn't wait to drink up to flush down a commode.

He started up Independence Avenue, staggering and muttering to himself, practicing the vagrantness strut he planned to adopt. He never would have believed it, had he asked himself the other day, but it honestly felt good playing the sober polite drunk, just so long as he pulled in five hundred that day. Made him a little salty though, being a coward about taking up them acting classes. He probably could have had one major acting career by now, had he not he flagged film school. Surely he'd be much better off than what ended becoming the case, trying to follow Pop's footsteps when clearly Pop was the last of the retiring breed.

A woman digging in her purse about to feed a meter caught his attention. With her purse hung open and she scrounging to the bottom of it, it looked like a fine opportunity to ask if she could spare some change.

"Ma'am...ma'am...please help a sick vet..." and he found himself also doing *the bounce*, just a little though, bumbling his way in front of her so that he couldn't be ignored. "Please...please...a dollar will do. So an old vet can get a cup of soup."

The woman didn't answer. She tried to pretend as if he wasn't there, shoving her face deeper in the purse. If she could just focus on the finding more coins, scraping the corners and all sides, *this thing* might leave her alone and go away.

But he didn't. The one thing he told himself when he drafted the plan, he had to be persistent, career advice he was given at Linthicum but ignored.

"You need to make yourself more visible," capital K.A.W., wrote in his evaluation.

"Why," he asked when K.A.W. finally crawled out from behind his shell for a face-off meeting to discuss why all year long he said nothing about him doing less than satisfactory work.

"Visibility is the key to a successful career," K.A.W told him, mimicking Linthicum's buzzwords. Linthicum could have written in a memo tucking his tail beneath his butt was the way to go, and he would have echoed that too. K.A.W, the spineless creature he was, was the typical walking infomercial for every corporation in America. The *Kiss-Ass-Wipe* prototype.

So he ignored the ill thought-out advice. He was just fine where he was. Even if he'd been told he was surfing a tidal wave, he would have rode that swell too. Better to be above the sharks than swimming with them. And now here he was, on level ground, where he controlled how persistent he wanted to be.

He expected the woman to go on ignoring him, or maybe spit in his face, but she surprised him. She came up with two bills crumpled together and mashed them into his hand and hurried down the street.

"Thank you ma'am…God bless you. God bless your soul." Happily he staggered on up the street thinking two dollars was even better than what he calculated. If he doubled his expectations, he might also end up with a doubly good book. He strolled assuredly on to his next casualty.

"Sir…sir…please help a sick vet…" and he did the bounce, adding a nod and a little saliva to the skit, wiping his mouth on the end of his sleeve. "Just anything you can spare to help an honorable vet with the cost for a cup of tea and some soup," going as far as to wipe the extra juice he let build up around his mouth on the end of both sleeves.

"You disgraceful prick," the man spat back. "You think I'm stupid! You worthless piece of scum! You need to be thrown beneath a cell for perpetrating a fraud." And he spat on his shoes!

'Oh God! His shoes!' He looked down and realized he must have left the running shoes in the car, or at home. His Bremen leather loafers were as polished and shined as two shoes could ever get. He lost his nerve, genuinely staggering over to a wall to brace himself.

'Come on Cliff, you can do it. You can't let a small set back like this get you down brotha. Think five hundred a day… five hundred tax-free dollars a day for just one year Cliff. That's all. You can do it brotha.'

That was the spill he was giving himself when a voice hit him from his blind side. "Hey, hey my man," came a flat raspy voice heated by so much funk he could feel scales warming the right side of his face. "You got anything you can let me hold?"

He turned his head to meet a crusty mouth and a hardened scabby hand held out in front of him. Those were this man's beauty traits. The pair of grape eyes juggling around like dancing puppets from the end of a string was the man's other side.

Any other day and he would most certainly have been shooing this person away. But this person was now him, in a peculiar, but real way. He didn't fear him, and neither pitied him, but in an errant wish to rethink what he was doing, he happened to look down at the man's feet. He swallowed hard. "Say, how about you trading me my shoes for yours?"

My man looked down at his feet, his eyes lighting up like Christmas. "Cool, cool my man. I like them there shoes," and he braced himself against the wall hurriedly kicking off a grubby pair of battered running shoes. By God did this man's feet stink. His feet smelled like a frightened skunk swimming among dead fish.

He squeezed his eyes shut trying to fend off the odor. There was no way he could stick his feet in those shoes. He wanted to rescind the offer, but it was too late.

The man was already out of the smelly shoes, nodding his head spasmodically looking towards the ground. Not all the drool trickling out of his mouth was due to the inability to close his mouth. He wanted the shoes so bad he could taste them.

Graciously Cliff turned over his shoes, shoes he wore countless times in to work, staring at them while KAWs talked progressive corporate talk about building bridges, knocking down walls, and trekking stepladders.

With his eyes squeezed tight as they could go, he slipped out of the loafers to trade his good KAW shoes for one miserable pair of funky running shoes. Any shoes were better than no shoes. October wasn't the best month to be walking around DC naked around the feet.

My man jumped right into his shoes and busily got on his way, snapping his fingers and spinning small doughnuts dancing down the street. "Hey, thanks my man! These shoes here feel real good," he called out in one last turn, arms raised high as if he'd hit the jackpot.

Nauseously Cliff again looked down at the running shoes My Man left behind. They looked so hot that a puff of steam seemed to be rising above them. Easing into the shoes he pictured stepping into marsh mixed of discarded eggs, cow gut, and vomit. His stomach even quibbled as he stepped into the left shoe. And he almost spilled his guts when he eased into the right shoe. When he got both feet in, squishing and sinking as he tried standing on his full weight, he realized he hadn't lost any parts of his stomach. Carefully he took a step, and then another, telling himself he could do it. A few more steps and he found himself creeping by a large glass window. Catching his reflection he thought he looked vagabond good. Like a perfect reflection of a man living on the streets. The shoes were an instant hit. The new pre-washed jeans and long flannel night-shirt hanging to his knees got along well with the squishy shoes.

Before long he was walking at a good clip, part of the way skipping and singing as well, not realizing it was almost noon and he had another four hundred and ninety-eight people to nudge out of a dollar, barely enough to pay the tickets accumulating on the meter he forgot to feed.

● ● ●

Merda got home first. She usually did. And just like she also usually did after arriving home, she went straight to his room to check to see if he'd locked his door. That morning he hadn't. He was so excited about his new venture he ran out of the house with just the briefcase.

The toeless black shoes he bought the other day sat in the middle of the floor in his bedroom. It was the first thing Merda noticed. She bent down and picked them up, examining how the toes were cut out of what looked like a brand new pair of…women's running shoes!

She knew it! She something was going on with Cliff. It just wasn't normal that a fifty-two year old man would never settle down and make a family.

"Have you seen these?" And she shoved the running shoes beneath Parker's nose.

He leaned back. No, he hadn't seen the running shoes. "What about them? Who's are they?"

"What about them!?! Who's are they!?! These belong to Satan! That's who!"

Parker looked up at her, dilemma-eyed, wishing for once she would mind her own business. Things were so peaceful when she wasn't seeing Satan. Why was she so bothered by Cliff? He wasn't. Cliff never bothered him.

He shook his head but tried to look concerned. One thing about Merda, she hated being ignored. At least she hated it when he ignored her. Others ignored her all the time. Or rather, they avoided her. She never refrained from involving herself in new mess and then wondered why everything had to be such a struggle. People who dealt with their own issues almost always freed up half of their problems. Like him. He was as free as a bird. He didn't have half the problems she did.

On her end, Parker was no help. She called her good

friend Theresa. They'd been friends a long time, since they were kids, talking about everything…church and godly things mostly. Never anything as embarrassingly sinful as what she was holding in her hands though.

"Do you think Cliff could be gay?"

"Well, you know he's always been a little strange." Theresa had known Cliff when he was in diapers, running around with the snotty noses and poop in his pants. She was the one who even got him a date for his senior prom. She got her cousin Jacqueline, who at first didn't want to go, but returned home talking about how nice and wonderful Cliff was.

"But cross-dressing!?! I'm not living with no cross-dresser! This is it! He's got to go!"

"Wait now… Have you asked him?" With all the writing Cliff did, the shoes could have meant anything. "What if he had a woman over visiting? The shoes could belong to her. Or, maybe he's role-playing?"

"So I should be looking out for a woman with ostrich toes!?!" Merda huffed. "Terry, I know these shoes belong to no one but Satan! They are brand new!"

Merda recounted the other day's events, him getting home before her and acting fishy out there in the yard fighting with her dogs. She ended up having to take both dogs to the vet after he near poisoned them with the ammonia he poured on garbage. The can where he, intentionally she was sure, hadn't tied down the lid. She tried hard not to believe that's what he did, and if he hadn't been her brother she would have turned him in for animal cruelty. It was no wonder why Dutchie and Echo didn't like him. They smelled the fish on him too.

But this cross-dressing business was another matter entirely, something she needed to take to church and pray on. Just to think what all this might be doing to her parents trying to be at peace in heaven. It was just too much to bear.

She threw the shoes out in the yard to Dutchie and Echo. Let them amuse themselves with a new chew toy. She was getting down on her knees to seek God's guidance. She opened her Bible to Revelations 5:5 and prayed, *"...And one of the elders saith unto me, Weep not...behold, the Lion of the tribe..."* she mumbled aloud, silently berating herself for calling him Satan. Pastor Edmonds only spoke on this matter the other Sunday... *"Keep the tongue from evil, and the lips from speaking guile. Depart from evil, and do good; seek peace, and pursue it,"* he preached.

But she wasn't thinking of Clifford at the time. She was thinking about some of the women in the church. Those bent on stirring up trouble, Mother Eloise mostly, and her sidekicks Sisters Madeline and Louise. They knew First Lady Leslie's boys were tyrants. But they sat right there and watched them boys cutting up kicking the back of the pew Elder Bosoms sat on. Elder Bosoms had every right to get up, in the middle of service even, and straighten those boys out. Had she been sitting on that pew, or even close, she would have done the same thing…the same way she straightened out Cliff that time he cut up singing all over Pearl. *Talking about it wasn't his fault! It wasn't him.* She straightened his tail out the minute he got in the house. He didn't have no troubles before, but he sure had some later. A sore behind. It was the last time he pulled that stunt again.

This was what sometimes infuriated her about Cliff. He just wouldn't do right. As a child he always got into things…a mischievous little brat he could be. Mama just had him too late. They couldn't do nothing to raise him right, though the good Lord knew she tried.

She kept on his little butt, staying on him about doing his homework and pulling his load helping out around the house, and making sure he stayed out of trouble. She wished she had been home when he started high-school. By that time his father must have been too old to help him learn how to be a man. But she would have found a way to show him.

She stayed on her knees, praying and seeking God's understanding, anxiously waiting to hear the garage lift. Soon as he walked in she was going to clear her mind.

Come up with all the excuses in the world, but only Christ had the final say. And Christ never intended for two men, or two women, to share one bed. Never. It was immoral, and it was a sin. And all be darn if he was going to embarrass her the way he had done that day he thought he could get up in front of the entire church and show out the way he did. Entertainers belonged on stage on Broadway. Not up on the altar serving God!

• • •

Clifford got back to the spot where he parked the car around the same time Merda found the shoes. While she inspected the shoes, he inspected his pockets. He barely pulled up a hand full of coins. His only pay for the day, he spent on a bottle of water. All of two dollars and .17 cents, of which the .17 cents included Canadian coins. The clerk didn't give him too much of a hard time. After she yelled at him for trying to slip off the foreign coins she told him to take his water and get out of the store, "and don't let me see you back in here AGAIN!"

Be-bopping on, feeling the spirit of his new gig, working into the shoes my man pawned off on him, he lost all kind of track of time. He forgot about driving into the city. And by the squish in the shoes, he forgot he even owned a car. All in his head was what was going on between his toes, and what his toes might look like once he stepped out of the shoes.

He made it up to a Metro underpass, couldn't recall the name of the building, but it was a white ashy building, the spot where he stopped to hang around a few guys hoping to pick up a better script. One of them, the one he learned was Blue, wanted to know where'd he been.

"I just got out," he said, going into his act. Didn't know how it came to him to say this, or if the guys would buy it, but the words came out nicely natural.

The tall one, the one they called Hagerstown, stood there inspecting him strolling over, almost as if he wanted to laugh, reading him like the flake he was.

"Awl man, dat ain't Deep. You thought that was Deep," laughed the one with no *visible* legs and one arm, making the chair he was sitting in spin.

Hagerstown smirked and Blue squinted. But Cliff didn't stop his act. Can't say it didn't take a lot of nerve, because it surely did. He had a lot of nerve smiling with all of his good, clean, brushed teeth, and strolling over to a few guys who knew the streets years better than him, suited up in his crisp new *dress for less* clothes.

"Who you?" Blue asked with this giant chip on his shoulder, mad because he wasn't Deep, but trying to join them as if he was.

The shoes had to have held some kind of magic. They even added a little cushion to his stagger as he did his bounce walking over to the trio. "Man, I remember you from the ward. We was in the ward together."

"Naw pimp. You don't know me," Blue said looking him dead in the face, his snarl upstaged by a tarnished capped tooth.

Clifford stopped smiling after that. He was still in his act. His role just needed tweaking a bit. "Man, you was out of it. I thought you wasn't gonna make it."

He didn't make it obvious, but beneath the act he counted the exact number of seconds that would pass before he'd know whether he was walking away or going to be carried away. Exactly five. If Blue didn't lay into him in exactly five seconds he just might make it out of there with at least one full chapter holding court and taking testimony from his hippocampus.

Slowly this ugly smile crept up on Blue's face. It turned up a corner of his mouth making the capped tooth look more deranged. "What? You a NARC or somethin'?" And he looked him up and down.

First, tell me if you got any drugs and then I'll let you know, he mused quietly. He didn't dare say this though. By his count, and he started recounting after Blue's answer, but he had only three more seconds to go. "Shit…they couldn't pay me enough…" Adding the *shit*, added authenticity. Without it, he was a NARC for sure. And a geeky one at that. At least that's how he felt.

He started walking away when an arm caught him around the neck from behind. He felt something hard and blunt poking him in the side. And he smelled Blue's breath.

"Where ya' boyz at? Where dey at? Let's see if they come out to save ya' ass," Blue breathed into his neck. It startled him for a second. He had only gotten all the way up to one in the count. But after that second, especially when Blue laughed loud in his ear, smacking him with a kiss in the ear too, did he relax.

"Ah ha! You ain't no damn NARC. How you know me? Was you in General?" Blue continued laughing with the watchful Hagerstown looking on, and Simp in his world still spinning them semi circles in the wheelchair.

"Yeah," he answered, sullen and thrown off key.

"Deez fools over here talkin' bout Steele is on our side. I say Steele ain't shit. What 'chew see?"

Hagerstown waited. Before he intently watched him. Now he openly dared him, challenging him to say more. Taxing him with that wily stare that said he'd been drinking since he was a child, hard 100% proof alcohol, eyes so red they looked pulled from a dragon and sewn into his face. But through the scarlet veneer was an astute glare that said he read him well.

Cliff looked at Blue good and hard, careful not to let Hagerstown's vilifying grin distract him, and coolly told him, "I don't know no Steele," and he turned to walk off.

He knew what happened when there was a crowd. He'd seen this bunch at Linthicum too many times. They huddled in groups and tested newcomer's spine and backbone. Too much of either and they would team up to break one or the other, or both. It was the only time he witnessed such a valiant effort of team camaraderie.

"Hey my man...where you headed off to," Blue apologized.

"Gone up to twenty-first," he tossed behind him, adding more bounce in his stride, thanking every harking angel that had come to his rescue.

"Awl Pimp, what's on twenty-first," Blue called after him. "Bring us back a sammich," he teased.

He kept bouncing, pacing his dips to how good he suddenly felt. *What were them fools doing talking politics anyway? What did they know about Steele and Pelosi?* He caught up to a man going by Roscoe not more than 500 yards from where he'd come...selling jewels. These weren't jewels of the Nile like rare blue diamonds and stuff like that. These were homemade crafts. Polished stones and pebbles drilled and fed onto thin wires. Roscoe called them his African collection. He'd been making and selling them for a few months, he explained.

"Well, what's this one here do," and he came up out of his pocket with a fist full of crumpled one-dollar bills. He had to show Roscoe he was serious about making a purchase, so he wouldn't get suspicious like Blue and Hagerstown. A part of knowing the streets was knowing the people. Beneath the canopy of dreadlocks and smell of incense Roscoe looked like a fairly serious dude that if he quickly connected with, he might protect him from dudes like Blue.

"These here are stones from Istanbul…brought them back after serving two tours in Turkey."

"Two tours in Turkey?"

"Yeah…what, you've been there?"

No, he hadn't. And had DC and Virginia not been so close, the furthest he could say he'd been was on the outer loop of the beltway…and Florida.

"That's a long way from home," he bounced, doing the nod and fumbling a cloth bangle that tied around the wrist. "I don't like flying, so I could have never gone so far away."

It was Roscoe's proudest moment. He had done something many men like him were afraid to do, plus he served his country, another thing most men were afraid to do. The proof he had displayed across an eight-foot table. He could tell him anything and he'd have to believe it.

"Did this come from Istanbul too," speaking of the cloth bangle he held in his hand.

"Yes my friend. Everything here is a product from Istanbul. That there comes from head wraps men and women wore back in the early 1800's." Roscoe leaned into Clifford inspecting the sturdy piece of textile. "See, that's raw silk," and then he admitted, "well, it's been treated to keep it from wearing, but it was worn by a spy who ultimately had been killed…"

Clifford immediately put the bangle back where it was and picked up one of the pebbled bangles. "What's this one do? I need something for luck!" He preferred the bangles that tied, they looked more masculine, but he would wear a garter belt, hosiery, and heels if it were the only choice between that and something a dead man, or woman had worn.

"Now that's your lucky piece right there!" Roscoe cheered, pulling his leg for sure. He didn't know any more about where those pieces came from than the little old Turkish man who gave them to him. The typical Rasta man. Trying to sound more worldly than the script called for.

"Great my man. I'll take it. How much is it?"

"For you my friend, just give me fifteen," Roscoe said like nothing, turning around to greet a family of tourists descending on the other end of the table.

"These are rare pieces from Africa," Roscoe greeted the tourists in his artificially robust voice. "Everything here has been handcrafted and is authentic," he beamed.

While Roscoe brazenly explained his rare jewels, Cliff peeled off fifteen dollars, money he left the house with, and waited for the presentation to end.

"Here you go my man," and he laid the crumpled bills on the table. "You've got some good stuff," and he peered the 500-yards back to where Hagerstown, Simp, and Blue were still cutting up. "It's too bad they don't have a clue," he nodded in the three men's direction.

Roscoe narrowed his eyes and looked too. "Yeah," he sighed, "war 'll do that to a man."

"Vietnam vets too, huh?" Clifford muttered, about to move on.

"Nam!?! Awl, no my friend. Those cats came out of the Storm!"

Clifford turned back around to get another look. The one in the chair with the blanket draped over his legs, Simp, even if he had all of his teeth in, looked no less than seventy. Hagerstown too. Height aside, to look in his eyes, how wise but tired they looked, he would have guessed he might have been hanging in the background of General Patton's crew. After that he had to face it. He wasn't no good at guessing ages. Note to himself: Laugh long, loud, and hard. After that, get plenty sleep.

"Them cats are out there rain and shine...every day," Roscoe murmured like a low-grade ache, keeping his eyes on them as if he was seeing down a tunnel into a long dark tragic loss. "The big cat used to be an LT before they demoted him and chaptered him out," he said sadly. "And the one in the chair ain't even thirty." He shook his head and turned away.

"Man," Clifford shook his head too. "Every day?"

"Yeah...every day they're out here. They're harmless though," he laughed, "long as they're on their meds."

Clifford walked on, the time marching in stride with his pep. It was the best feeling ever. Like he had closed his eyes and jumped into a pool, both feet first, twenty feet deep. A day ago, when he was the man in the suit walking by, these people were the ousted he hoped didn't sit next to him on a train, or ask him for spare change, or who he'd shoo off his windshield, wishing they somehow would vanish. They were the lowest common denominator the world had to offer. But that was then, before moving into their world, standing beside them, watching their eyes, reading their thoughts, feeling and smelling their breath, and trading them for shoes and phony authentic jewels.

He made his way to a coffee shop, hankering in this good mood, where he spent more money feeling like the richest man in the world. He wished he had brought a book with him, but then tossed that thought when he accidentally overturned his tea spilling the hot liquid in his lap. That was another sign. Something was about to open his eyes and change his life forever.

Busily attending to the spill he looked over a few tables and caught sight of the most lovely goddess in the world. She was so faint in features he had to block out the trees shading her expression to find her face. This was the woman he'd spent all of his life searching for, and didn't even know it.

To one side of her sat a triplet of trashcans and on the other side of her was a shopping cart filled with dark green lawn-size trash bags. She seemed to be looking his way though he couldn't tell for sure. Her eyes, absorbing the shade and moving with the breeze, looked to be seeing through a vacillating stare.

Quickly he grabbed his things, an empty Styrofoam cup and a paper sack containing the other half of his bagel, and hastily moved towards her, gallantly on an empty thought. She could have been committed, taken, or but a mirage of imagined lust, and none of this was worth considering.

"Hello darling," he smiled, thumping the tray on the edge of a trashcan. "Nice weather we're having, huh?" He didn't feel like a fool running the lamest pick-up line in creation to use on her. The woman deserved the best.

She smiled back, feebly, and went back to staring off in the distance.

"On a clear day they say you can see far," he stood in front of her, watching her, waiting to see if he could catch her taking her next breath. Before the layoff he would have never had the nerve to walk up to a woman with his intentions and lay these sorrowful lines down on a beauty as stunning. But *she* was different. He could tell by the way she ignored him. His presence neither bothered her, nor alarmed her. She took him in like she took in the gentle zephyr dipping her thoughts in that far out place where he longed to one day share.

But for good measure he wanted to wake her. "You wanna shack up with me?" Now this was his best pick-up line. Not only was it lame, desperate, and absurd, but it was obvious, salient, precise, and the surviving sword he had left to get her attention.

"I'm doing just fine," she shyly giggled.

See, he was in. Without wasting a beat, he pulled out a chair and sat at the table beside her. "My lady, I can see you're doing just fine, but my question is would you like to live with me?"

Honestly, he was dead serious. Looking at her fragile slim fingers, thin shoulders, delicate face, and watching her face flush and blush he meant every word. He wasn't leaving without her consent.

"So what do you say," he persisted.

"Where do you stay," she meekly giggled.

"Oh, just in an old big house a little piece from Tacoma Park," he smiled as if answering a young child.

"Tacoma Park," she brightened up, still with the squeaky giggle attached however. "What are you doing all the way over here!?!" If a tangerine could talk, he imagined they would sound alike. Sweet and tangy.

"I'm out scouting for a woman to share my life with and I believe I've found her," he smiled.

The thing was, he could freely admit this. He wasn't up against any competition impeding his feelings. No other woman, at least not when he was with Linthicum, would he have dared to be as open and forthright with. They would have laughed at him, blown him off, told all their friends, who later would've laughed at him again. He just wouldn't have scrounged up the nerve.

But it was what he felt at the moment. It was what he wanted. Truly wanted. It was what his soul told him he needed to say. If he hadn't said these things he was sure he'd lose her.

The lady didn't answer. And she stopped giggling and blushing. She sat there staring at him, for the first time looking at him.

"Miss Lady, I'm serious…well…" and he moved into a spot he hadn't rehearsed. Actually, not much he'd said or done that day had been rehearsed. Most of it was off the cuff and off script. But this was a different off the script. A feeling had crept up inside him and he was running with it. He could tell this lady was no push over. She didn't run off with anyone at the drop of a hat. She had principles. She had to carefully search his face and think on this one for a minute.

"...the truth is, I really came out here to see if I could make five hundred bucks a day panhandling—"

"—five hundred dollars!?!" she shrieked, quenching. "...A day!?!" She shrieked again, laughing in his face. "Man, you some kind of fool if you think you can make five hundred a day out here." But then she looked at him with the warmest smile, though by the tilt of her head she was still asking if he was he was really serious. He sounded serious, and looked serious, but nah...he couldn't be serious.

"...If that much could be made, no one would have to work? All these buildings," and she fanned around, tiny hand waving through the air, "...all these shops you see would be dress shops," she laughed.

Cliff nodded. He thought the same thing too. His ambitions just happened to be a little higher than his thoughts. If he worked hard at it, anything was possible though. At least that's what one of his Linthicum KAWs told him.

"Well, how much do you think I can make?" The woman obviously must have had verifiable proof. She certainly sounded more convinced than him.

"A few cups of tea or coffee if you're lucky," she continued chuckling, tickled to tears at the concept.

"Okay then…so what's the most you've ever made?"

"Aah," and she looked up to the sky thinking back. "One time I got fifty dollars…but…" she interjected, "…that was just from one person," and her mood glided just like that into a tailspin spiraling outward. She didn't want to talk any longer about why the person gave her fifty dollars. It took her to a bad spot, a place where she didn't care to venture. When Clifford tried to coax it out of her she completely shut down. The light inside of her, just like that, died out.

"Okay then…if you won't tell me, at least let me prove to you what my house looks like." Merda would probably kill him, but did he care? He'd probably kill her back. This was the woman he wanted to share the second half of his life with. This was the heroine of his next romance novel. *My Dearest Love*.

"Mister, I'm really fine just where I am."

"Miss Lady, I already told you I can see that. But what's it gonna to hurt if for one day, at least, you get to visit someplace you've never been?" He changed his voice, and played with his eyes trying to nosedive into her heart, aiming at getting her to laugh again. "I'm a real good cook," and he winked. "I'll make you a nice home-cooked meal, and run you a nice long hot bath, bubbles too," he teased, "and let you sleep in my big warm fluffy bed…"

"With you in it I bet," she grimly retorted.

He lifted up, disappointed. "Awl, come on… Look, I'm not trying to take advantage of you. I really want to prove to you I mean what I say." And he looked around hoping to come up with something more convincing.

"I don't even know your name," she prudently shot back. "How am I supposed to know if you're not Jack the Ripper coming back to life!?!"

"Miss Lady," and he stood, bowing in front of her, "you are absolutely right. Please accept my apologies. My name is Cliff-Clifford Maurice Blanchard, and I have nothing to hide from you. Now, what is your name?"

He thought she said Debbie, but her name turned out to be Tebby, even prettier. Offering him her name had to imply consent, so he held out his hand and thought he would drop to his knees when she accepted. Felt like he held nothing but a few branches of straw fresh off a smoldering fire in his hands.

"Here, let me get that," stepping between her and the shopping cart she also reached for. "You have a man now. No more heavy lifting and pushing for you."

He was far ahead of himself but no longer cared. She didn't seem to mind either. They walked a short distance away to where she'd been staying in a hotel for drifters. About ten tenants lived in the hotel, leasing space on the upper floors above a restaurant. For only ten dollars a day they got a full kitchen and a bedroom. The lavatory facilities were shared. One for each floor.

Just as expected it was clean up there, but shoebox small. One thing he couldn't figure out, and that was why she walked around with a shopping cart full of her belongings when she had somewhere to stay.

She got him good with that pondering. Teased by a small smile and an oblique wink, she told him she was a professional panhandler too.

That's how the day shot by so fast. He had forgotten all about needing to feed the meter. Unlike what he recalled being the case at Linthicum, watching the clock like a hawk, seeing every second tick by in a slow agonizing drawl, this day breezed by. He couldn't wait to get home and write. It was a good chance he could have his love story written by the end of the week.

"Where you from," Tebby asked, sweeping her thoughts over the pavement as they headed towards K Street, where he parked.

"Well…let's see…I was born in Chow, Maryland. Attended Howard for two years—"

"—you went to Howard!?!"

"Yes, I did," he answered officiously, quickly settling her curiosity explaining how many hustlers were college educated also.

"I know that," she rowed back, bringing the giggle back as well. "I went to Howard too!"

Surprised by the admission but holding his ground he fought her on it, "you went!?! ...you mean you're still going don't you!?!"

"Them people too snooty for me. I had to get out of there before they got me like them," she offered, clearly ignoring his insinuation.

They fell into a silent stride for a while, her sandals lightly clapping against the ground and his burdened breaths taking head on the buzz swelling his chest and filling his head. Nothing could squeeze between this buzz, except maybe visualizing her riding with him...to his home, until the meter he forgot to feed dawned on him. The windshield probably was going to be plastered with tickets. *Oh well, whatever it cost him, would be well worth it. There was always the next day to prove what Tebby said was impossible, was possible. She seemed like a fun-loving lady. She could even help show him all the best parts to work.*

They walked up one side of K Street, and down the other, and around a curvature corner. Cars parked back to front lined the street, but his car wasn't there.

"I can't believe this," he muttered, "…someone stole my damn car!"

Tebby looked up at the sign screwed to a pole they stood beside. "Cliff, how long have you been here?"

Hands on his hips, looking around anguished, trying to figure out what next, he answered in that haze. "Since this morning…" and then cautiously retracing his steps, thinking back, "…I remember parking right here in front of these…"

"…Cliff," Tebby quietly said. "*They* towed your car."

CHAPTER ...5

Bitter Hench Men & Towing was the least of his concerns. He and Tebby hailed a cab. Or more like they snatched a cab. The first few he tried to stop drove by. Light on, cab empty, the cabbies took one look at him, and Tebby, and stepped on the gas.

"The nerve of these towel head evangelists!" They'd been in the country all of a few days and already trying to bring back slavery. But then a black African flew by them too. Same thing. Light on, cab empty and the black man gassed it. He whipped out a credit card, Tebby standing behind him just a giggling, and another one flew by. "Okay, watch this," he tells Tebby. "The next one won't stand a chance!"

He grabbed Tebby's hand and walked near a couple who'd just left the hotel. They were hailing a cab too. The broad shouldered white man dressed in a suit, and his lovely companion dressed in a dinner dress. Sure enough a cab came racing up the street, light on, cab empty, and stopped dead on the dime right at the lovely couple's feet. The broad shouldered brood went to open the door when Clifford met him beside the cab.

"Sir, my wife and I were out here first. Do you mind letting us have this cab? I'm sure another one will stop for you a lot quicker than for us."

As the cab driver looked behind, snatching around from left to right trying to get a good glimpse of what was going on, the woman whispered to her companion and both stepped aside. The cabbie didn't like it and struggled climbing out of the cab. "Get out! I'm taking them!" the cabbie angrily shouted at him and Tebby, arms flailing and spit flying up and down, left and right.

"Cliff, let them have it," Tebby pleaded. The cabbie eyes were so inflamed it looked as if someone had set them on fire.

"No!" And he leaned forward through the partition and snapped a picture of the cabbie's credentials.

"What are you doing!?! Get out! Get out!" The cabbie cried, reaching inside for the radio.

But the broad shouldered man stopped the cabbie. He tapped him on the arm and told him they no longer wanted to ride with him. "Please, take them and go!"

The cabbie drove wildly, angry as a hornet, running stoplights and turning corners on two wheels, the tires screeching and squealing as he raced them to the garage. And still it was a ride in ultra paradise, Tebby holding onto him the way she was and him imagining they were on a theme ride, lights and screams peeling around them as he wrapped his arms around the only woman he ever loved…to protect her.

• • •

"Where in the hell have you been!?!" That was Merda standing at the door, hand on hip and a dozen or so large curlers haphazardly hanging on to pieces of her hair. Steam ballooned around her, making her look more like a cartoon character than a real life person.

"You aren't my mother and you aren't my wife. I don't owe you anything!" He grabbed Tebby by the hand and brushed by her, heading to his room.

"Cliff, you know this isn't right," she cried as he passed by. "And take off your shoes! You know we don't wear shoes in the house!"

It was an out of body experience walking Tebby to his room with Merda nipping at their heels, until he shut the door in her face. Although he had women in his room before, he hadn't invited anyone over since Merda moved back home. And out of everyone that visited him, no one near to Tebby's quality had been in his room. The few friends he had, and he couldn't even call them friends since he saw them once or twice a year, it was usually at their place that he visited.

Like an out of body experience, similar to how he felt when he first left for college, dropping in on a new world, coming and going as he pleased, no one to hassle him about right and wrong, or chastise him about missing classes, or watch his every move, Tebby being in his room felt liberating. As if he'd stepped in the middle of a dream come true and was lounging on cloud nine.

"Cliff, are you sure it's okay for me to be here," Tebby whispered after he locked the door.

"Of course. This is just as much my house as it is hers. In fact, it's more of my house since I pay all the bills," he gushed, feeling like eighteen again.

This wasn't written in the script either. He could have never guessed he would meet a woman like Tebby.

Had he seen Tebby in the picture, things would be going far different. Merda would have long ago been out of the picture. There wouldn't have been a door to shut in her face. Other than the front door.

"Let me show you around," he smiled, guiding her by the arch in her back like the princess she had become to him. "This in here," and he opened the door beside his bed, "is my lovely sitting and writing room."

She poked her head inside the room he jazzed up with for reading; a recliner for musing, and his writing table equipped with every gadget from a typewriter, to laptops, and PC. The library she couldn't see.

"When I hit this switch," and he flipped the light switch midway, "we get music," he grinned as Bach's cello filled the room.

"You like that?"

She smiled too, her eyes twinkling as she looked around the room, and up over the ceiling.

"You can't see the speakers huh?"

And she shook her head no.

"Come on, I have one more thing to show you." He guided her to the opposite side of the room, giddy with excitement anticipating the new twinkle he would see when she saw the bathroom. He slid the door open and watched her face shrink. It was hardly the reaction he expected. "What's wrong? You don't like it?"

"It's fine Cliff," and she turned towards him. "I just don't understand why you have to be beggin' when you have all of this."

"Sssh," he put a finger to his lips. She wasn't loud. He just wanted to be sure she knew it was their secret. "My sister doesn't know I lost my job today," he said. "If she finds out, she could have me evicted."

It was a little too much for Tebby. Meeting a stranger who takes her from one setting to bring her to something new, was like taking Cinderella from the dungeon to the ballroom in a pumpkin and her losing a shoe.

"Do you want to try the hot tub out?" He nudged her with a small nod. "I'll get you some towels and get you all set up."

"Cliff, I don't think I'm ready for this…" she paused, "I mean—"

"—Tebby…Tebby…" and he kissed her forehead. Gosh, she smelled so sweet, like she hardly needed a bath at all. "Darling…Miss Lady…I am not going to take advantage of you. I already told you this…I promise."

He opened his closet and brought out a plush towel set, gold, and laid them on the bed. "I'm going in my haven," pointing to his sanctuary, "take your time and get comfortable. I don't want to force you to do anything you don't want to." Another thought hit him. "Hey, do you like to read?"

She smiled wide then. "Yes, actually I do."

"Welp…" and he turned the light switch inside his sanctuary to its full position. "Look."

She walked inside the room to face the wall she missed just peeking in. Her mouth fell open. "Oh my God…" she mouthed… "It's wonderful," and she moved closer to touch the books.

"Take your time…browse all you want…" slipping into his writing chair and firing up his PC. "I'm about to get into my zone…" he laughed, "to start working on our story…"

• • •

"Cliff! Cliff!" She yelled like the house was on fire.

He rolled off the couch and stumbled to his feet, dazed, looking around for the flames, wondering if he'd soon be choked by the smell of smoke. A few seconds later he realized it was Merda yelling like that.

Stumbling to the door he unhinged the latch and unlocked the deadbolt and peaked out. "What is it?"

"It's eight o'clock. You're late!"

It took another moment for it to sink in and register what he was late for. Work, though there was no work. "I already called out…but thanks," he mumbled, again closing the door in her face.

He slid beneath the covers and snuggled up to the pillow closet to him so groggy it didn't click that Tebby was beneath the covers too. It felt like every other time he called out, trying to bury his face in the pillows to block the jagged stream of sunlight pouring through the window. It took a grunt to erase Merda from his from his thoughts and a slight shift getting comfortable before he realized there was a foreign object in bed with him.

Tebby! And he threw the comforter back and sprung out of bed as if he thought he felt a snake crawling up his leg. It had been a long time since he hopped up that quick. He was a good forty pounds lighter, and leaner, and played volleyball half the day. He was lucky he landed on both feet.

Nestled in bed with the comforter pulled over her head, she didn't budge. All that weight making the bed bounce and quake as he tumbled to his feet, and nothing else moved. She had to be a pretty hard sleeper to sleep through that, and the yelling too.

He started to wake her, to make sure she was okay, when the covers moved. "Hey, are you awake in there," he whispered, careful not to alarm her by touching her.

She didn't respond. She lay so defiantly still that it dawned on him something could be wrong. He debated waking her. *What if she had stopped breathing during the night? Would someone suspect old strange Cliff of foul play?*

Merda likely would, before and after she prayed on it. The thought frightened him. He should have thought better of bringing a transient home and letting her sleep in his bed. Merda would have every bit of evidence to prove his lack of sound judgment. Heck, he could've been wrong in thinking this was love at first sight. It wouldn't have been the first time, even if this time he was sure he felt different.

Holding his breath and praying, he waited, staring so intently at her contour that he got to thinking about witchcraft. He could pull back the covers and find more than a lifeless body beneath the comforter. She could lift up and be a three-headed unicorn, or worse, a three-headed transvestite unicorn.

Pacing around the bed he tried to think of the best way to wake her and alleviate his growing concerns. He suddenly was in a big hurry to see her lift up and open her eyes.

Opening and closing drawers as loudly as he could without slamming them, he kept watching the covers, waiting for movement. Whoever he brought home really was a hard sleeper.

He figured he better shower, to clear his head, hoping and praying that when he stepped back into the room Tebby would be the Tebby he brought home and dreamt of all night.

"Oh, so I see we're up," he sighed when he entered the room to find her sitting in the center of the bed with her knees drawn up to her chin and arms locked around her legs. He couldn't tell how long she'd been sitting there like that, but it was a pleasant relief to walk up on. With the small face but large eyes, she looked like a schoolgirl on her first camping trip looking at him the way she was.

"What's that," she asked, pointing somewhere near his midsection.

He looked down on the old battle scar he tried to cover with a tattoo he had since removed. "Oh, that," he laughed sheepishly embarrassed. "Yeah, that's just a childhood prank. I was trying to find myself and wound up in a tattoo parlor."

"You're a strange man, Cliff," she laughed back. "I never met no one like you."

"And I never met no one like you…pretty as you are. Anyone tell you how pretty you are?"

Bashfully giggling, she buried her face between her knees. "How would someone know to tell me that," and she fell back on the bed drawing the covers over her face. "I'm not pretty. I'm too old to be pretty."

He slid on the bed beside her, careful not to slide too close. "So, how old is old?" She certainly wasn't acting old, giggling the way she was. "*Say*…are you ticklish?"

She popped upright. "No! Don't tickle me," scaring him a bit, drawing him even further away. "I have to use the bathroom," and she slid the other way out of bed.

Just a few short minutes ago he was kicking himself for letting a stranger sleep in his bed and now, as she slinked by like a whisper, the overly long and too big night-shirt draped down to her knees, he was back at congratulating himself on the treasure he found. He guessed she was no more than thirty. Probably still in her twenties.

• • •

"Thirty-five! No way!"

"Yes way…" she smiled, dipping a strawberry into a bowl of whipped cream before sucking on it. She didn't know how seductive it looked, twirling the strawberry around the bowl and playing with the whipped cream the way she was, but if a camera was on her, she'd be one giggle away from an erotic film.

"You're just trying to make me feel good."

That's what he loved about her most. This innocence. Any woman who didn't realize sucking on a strawberry after dipping it in whipped cream wasn't teasing, had a lot to learn. All she had to do was look beneath the table and she'd get her first lesson.

"Why would I want to do that?"

"Because you want to get in my pants."

There it was again! The virtue. Who would openly admit to such a thing? "If I wanted to get in your pants, I'd already be in your pants." The greatest lie yet told. But it was what the script called for.

"Okay…I'm done," pushing the bowl towards him and brushing her hands together.

"No, please…have some more. I like watching you eat. I like the way your lips curl around the strawberry."

"Cliff, you're a strange man…"

"I know," he laughed. "You told me that already."

If she was thirty-five, then he was five, however the math worked out. Because of her, not so much as one paragraph came out of this new adventure. He sat up all night playing Star Wars, dreaming up desert islands, and tormenting himself trying to kill off all the life on the island so that he and her would be stranded. He played the game until he fell off the chair—asleep.

"Why are you staring at me like that?"

"Because I'm painting a picture…" and he draws an outline using the space between them as his canvas to trace the arches of a bell. "I'm seeing our life, framed, you and I. I'm going to write our story."

An original love story was what he had in mind. He wasn't exactly sure how he would begin, but its contents would writhe in passion. Like *Lawrence of Olivia*, or *Bridges of Madison*. Something romantic to conquer racial barriers, and social barriers, traverse continents, staying on the hearts and minds, lips and tongues of all who read it. Out last life, if that was possible.

But Tebby was skeptical. "How you gonna write a story about us when you don't even know me?"

"All I need to know is sitting right before me."

"Yeah," and she made no pretense of the fact that she was challenging him. "...Well, how is this story going to go?"

Okay, so she got him. He had no clue how the story would either begin or end. What he ran wild with was the middle...her and him meeting, and how infatuated he was by her blatant genuine aura.

"We don't need to know all of that right now. You just need to know that it's going to be breathtaking."

Tebby leaned back, and for the first time looked like a real person. Before she almost had this ghostly quality, as if he reached over and tried to touch her, she would disappear.

"Cliff, stop fooling around with me. You just sittin' over there making stuff up," waving his comment away. "You don't have no story cookin'..." she laughed.

For the clever lady she was showing herself to be, he closed his eyes and began reciting what he saw. "She came by a white knight, trimmed of fashionable coils, buttons, dear zibellinis, and orange blossoms in her hair. Trite to the touch, demur on the vision, he batted not an eye, nor wasted a notion to carrying her away…" and he stopped there, opening his eyes to see her staring at him, not as if she were waiting on more, but as if she was unsure if he were a titan or a duke.

"I know you don't understand it from just one verse, but—"

—but she interrupted him, so obviously she'd been following along. "Cliff, you got to have more than that. Me showing up on a horse? You didn't meet me on no horse. And how's this thing going to end?"

And so obviously she saw the same picture he had. "It doesn't matter how it ends. The beginning can be the ending, or the ending can be our beginning."

"Ah, no…I don't think I like this idea…you writing a story about me with no ending."

"But it's not going to be about you," he pleaded. "It's going to be about us…" and he took his time conjuring up an old *Dirty Harry-Charlton Heston* look, lowering his voice and dipping one brow. "It's going to be about a never-ending love fest of two people falling hopelessly and endlessly in love…"

"Love fest? Illlll…no…that don't sound so good to me," she giggled. "That sounds too creepy."

"Okay then...what do you suggest?"

"I suggest we know each before you go writing some book. Have you ever even written a book?"

He had. The book didn't make a big splash, in fact it sold fewer than 5000 copies, the reason both his agent and publisher dropped him. There wasn't much of a market for vampire stories, even if he had a producer in his back pocket who wanted to see the novel adapted to screen. But the producer ran out of capital and had to back out.

"You looked at it last night..." he winked, elated at the chance of entrapping her. "You didn't notice my name on the cover?" his turn to smile wide watching her scramble to think back.

"I was wondering why that book looked so strange," she shrugged, downplaying her surprise.

"You like me? Don't you?"

Again he trapped her, and he enjoyed every moment watching her recoil in thought.

"Cliff, I just don't think them stories sound like love stories to me."

"I bet you would make a good publishing agent."

She looked at him, wrinkling her nose, which didn't wrinkle very much. "Why you say that?" which she asked more like a statement, rather than a question.

"Because...you know what will and won't sell."

"I didn't say it won't sell," she objected. "I said it don't sound like no love story to me," leaving no trace that she was teasing him.

The burning ache that had crawled down his cheeks to his throat began to warm his heart. What a great answer. The abiding chaperon he'd always been seeking but didn't know where to look.

Turned out she knew her way around novels. Nora Roberts and McNaught were her favorites among the romance genre. He hadn't read them but felt like he had fallen into the mouth of a sinkhole, dropping out of his thoughts into hers, clumsily clutching onto her belief that strong heroines made better stories. The pacing was better, so she said. He asked about Jane Austen too, just to test her, himself knowing nothing of Austen's work either.

"How you gonna write a love story and you don't know Austen!?!" She said this after turning the question back on him, *'What did he think of Austen?'* But other than small rumors, Austen emerging as a controversial writer in the day and time she wrote, he didn't think anything, because he didn't know anything.

"Easy," he answered, enamored by her enthusiasm, and this great fervor to whip on his work by her own adroit knowledge of writing. "I'm writing about us and then I'm going to cloak the story."

"Cloak?"

"See, you don't know about that writing style," and he explained what cloaking meant. She still looked at him sideways, but refrained from challenging him. After all, she loved *The Time Machine*, but found *Rendezvous with Rama* troubling, just the opposite for him. He wasn't as smitten with a story, as he was with detailed writing. They went back and forth like this all morning. Her liking it hot, and him preferring it cold.

This hot and cold business leaked into to him telling her about his stalled writing, how he'd been working on several novels, not any anywhere near finished with any of them. He left out the nearly completed novel about Merda though. He wasn't up for the challenge on that one, especially since she hadn't taken to the term cloak.

"My writing flows better when I use the command of 18th century language…I think most people don't really read words for each word anyway. They just like to see them flowing on paper."

"Well, not me. I get seasick seeing too much of that flow. It's like watching a piece of paper float."

He couldn't help but laugh, though he was satisfied they had a story, however it was told. "I know what," and he reached across the table grabbing both her hands, "What do you say we write our story together," his grandest idea yet.

This time she didn't pull away, although she wasn't looking him in the eye either. "I don't know nothing about writing, Cliff. Just cause I read them don't mean I want to write them."

He wasn't convinced. Every bone in those little tiny fingers told him there was a heroic novel hiding out in those hands. She just lacked faith, wasn't giving herself credit where credit was due. "Tebby, you have to help me. This is the story I've been waiting on all my life."

"Awl Cliff, you're bright. God'll let you know when the time is right."

If he had a penny for every time that line crossed his path he'd already be reading about himself, instead of carving precious hours out of his life pleading his worth to apathetic agents.

"Did your mother name you Tebby, or is that your street name?" It'd been something he had been meaning to ask since she first told him her name.

"Why? You don't like my name? Are you making fun of my name, too, Cliff?"

"I love your name," and he reached across the table for her hand again, just to see her blush. "I've never heard of a name as unique and beautiful…"

She turned down her eyes as she looked away. "My name is Tabitha," she whispered. "My granddaddy gave me that name. Said I reminded him of his mother."

"I knew it was something special behind that name. Your granddaddy must have been a great man."

Abruptly she looked up alarmed. "Why do you say that," the sweet pitch running along.

"Because any granddaddy who'd name his granddaughter such a beautiful name has to be great."

"Well, he's the one that brought me into this world and raised me, so he ought to have named me," she spat angrily. "I hated my granddaddy."

He waited for her to say more but she never did. She found that small closet she'd been hanging out in and curled up inside.

"Why did your sister want us to remove our shoes?" That had been her burning question. She never heard of such a thing, except for in prayer books where people were doing it for religious reasons.

"She's a nut," he said dismissing the query, eager to find another spot where Tebby might let him probe.

"No Cliff...there has to be a reason. Something like that has to be done for a reason."

"All right...then she's a clean freak nut."

"Cliff, what sign were you born under," she asked as if the answer to the question would explain everything.

"I don't have a sign," he teased, testing his humor. "I was born in a month that isn't on the calendar. You have to get an archaic calendar."

She batted the remark away, surprising him giving in so easily. "When are you taking me home…it's almost four o'clock!"

He hadn't notice the time. Though the sunlight still peeping through the windows started to look old, he hadn't looked at the clock once. In fact, he had to look around when she told him, looking for the clock. Could she have asked anything besides that? Didn't she want to know how old he was? If he had a girlfriend, or *maybe ask if he wanted to kiss her*?

That question hurt. "I'm not," he said in his spooky voice. "You're mine…I'm keeping you here with me forever," he tried scaring her.

"Cliff, you better get your buns up and take me back home. I can't stay here forever!"

• • •

He had to make sure she wasn't doing him like Mr. Keller had done him when he was a child. Everyone called Mr. Keller, Reverend Kelly, everyone but him. To him he was always Mr., because that was the way Mr. Keller introduced himself.

"Hey there young man," Mr. Keller said early one Saturday morning from his front porch. "How would you like to rake Mr. Keller's front lawn for one dollar?"

A dollar back then was like twenty dollars to a small kid forty years later. So "sure," he said, and Mr. Keller showed him to the back of the house where the gardening tools were kept. He raked the lawn, and swept the steps, and back then Mr. Keller had a furnace in his kitchen he used to sweep out as well. Pleased with his work, Mr. Keller told him what a fine job he'd done and a fine boy he seemed to be, and invited him to stop by for lunch, *"anytime he felt like it."*

Thinking nothing of the good money he earned, or subsequent visits when Mr. Keller also made him fat sandwiches piled with enough lettuce, tomatoes, and meat to make five more sandwiches, he casually told Mama about the visits.

"Mr. Keller?" his mother curiously asked. She knew everyone on the block, and to her recollection, unless someone knew she moved in, there was no Mr. Keller.

He described the house, and the man, getting a little indignation in his tone that his mother was having so much trouble knowing who he was talking about. The man only lived a few doors away.

"Reverend Kelly!," his mother shouted when it came to her who he was describing. The enclosed porch was the cinch that clinched it. "Don't you accept another anything from that man! He paid you for one job, so now leave him alone," and she paused here, about to walk off when that thing that everyone else talked about but he didn't know, hit her. "And don't you stop and say nothing to that man ever again!"

Of course he ignored her. She never told him why. Plus, Mr. Keller always seemed to catch him when the streets were its quietest, usually Sundays when everyone was at church…another thing that confused him.

But he disregarded it all; the why Mr. Keller never seemed to go church…why he was called reverend… and why he was so insistent about sharing these fat delicious sandwiches with him, most times sitting together right there behind his enclosed porch.

Years later he found out what was going on. Mr. Keller was trying to win back the community by having him running back to the kids, telling them about how much money he made and the big delicious sandwiches he was feeding him. The thing was, he wasn't like most kids. Other than Mama, no one knew nothing about the money or sandwiches. And the only lesson to come out of it, for Mr. Keller eventually found his way back into the good grace of the community, but for Cliff, he hated the secrets. Why couldn't Mr. Keller have just been upfront with him? Why go through all of that trouble?

He tried to be as upfront as he could with Tebby, and hoped she was doing the same with him. He didn't want any secrets. He wanted her to trust him as much as he wanted to trust her. If she had children somewhere, or another social interest, or anything material he should know, he wanted to know.

"Cliff, I don't know how to keep any secrets," she told him. "You the one keeping secrets…"

"How's that?" He was sure he told her everything. He was single, had no children, and had never been married. What else could he have hidden up his sleeve?

"Well, I still don't understand why you want to go out beggin' with all of this."

• • •

A week later Tebby was still there, and Merda he found up on the roof peeling away cinder and tar with her bare hands. Not literally, but figuratively, she ripped through Parker's left ear, and then tore out Theresa's right ear, and careened through Tabernacle's Sunday morning services with a prayer that implored the church pray for her brother…and her.

Something had gotten into Clifford. First it was the cross-dressing. Now he robbed a cradle, stopped going to work, and was hiding this *poor* child in his room. There was no telling what was all else was going on in his mother's house, rest her soul, but something had to be done. Please pray for her.

And so, his soul beyond redemption, the church prayed. Her closet friends prayed, the neighbors prayed, and the family started dropping by, one by one, to see if they could catch a glimpse of the cradle Cliff robbed.

All week these innocent bystanders, troublemakers, and otherwise interested nosey rumor-makers grazed the front room on many pretenses; dropping off custard pies (Mrs. Grant knew those were his favorite…drawing him out the room every time, except this time). Sylvia stopped by to check in on Parker; the first time she thought to do so since they moved in. He doubted if she ever even met Parker. And there were others, many others, namely Theresa who he overheard telling Merda, *"well, at least he isn't gay!"*

The remark turned his ears a coal bitter burning red. How could Merda be telling these people these things? He looked over at Tebby, nuzzled in his favorite reading chair, a royal ancient lounge chair with a high back and velour cushions that seemed to swallow her whole. She was reading, one leg crossed over the other, oblivious to the chatter going on in the next room.

"Is he in there now," he heard Mrs. Grant whisper in her lovely hoarse voice.

"Yeah…he's back there," Merda cued Mrs. Grant in, in her shrill cackling unmusical tone. "Go ahead," she instigated, "go on back there and knock on the door."

Mrs. Grant knocked on the door, heavy-handed, startling Tebby to look up.

He did what he'd been doing ever since the eavesdropping started. He ignored the knock, swooning over Tebby to see how far she'd gotten in reading his novel.

"So where are you now," he swooped over her, looking over her shoulder to check the page.

"Cliff," Tebby squealed, singing his name in a note he found as arresting as the curl of her lips and how comfortably she looked enveloped in the chair. "Would you let me finish…and go see who's calling you at the door."

It was the last thing he wanted to do. He heard Mrs. Grant behind him, howling out his name in her hoarse rattle, "Cliff, come on out here…I made you some custard…haven't seen you in a month!"

That was a nice big flipper. Tebby had only been there a week. The week before that week he drove by her house every day going to and from work. Sometimes they waved at each other, sometimes they didn't. Not once however did she stop him, to offer one of her custard pies. On occasions she'd drop a pie or two after Sunday service, when she had made so many of them that she had to give them away, but even then they rarely exchanged more than a stiff hello as he came out to collect one of the pies.

He turned on the water at the kitchen sink up to its full power and rummaged through shelves to decide on what delicacy he could make for lunch. He had in mind Spinach dip over one of his special crouton salads. But he looked up in the cabinet and found he was all out of croutons.

"Cliff, why you ignoring them people?"

"Because they're spirit eaters," he said over running water. "Hey, I know! How about after they leave, you and I go catch a movie?"

"To see what?," and she turned a page with this sneaky grin on her face.

He had nothing in mind, except to get out of the house. So much for the five-hundred a day, they hadn't been out very much with him trying to avoid Merda. Twice they had gone to visit Tebby's friends, people she routinely looked after. It was a surprising treat, seeing how she spent her days, but he hoped for something a little more intimate where he could tease the chemistry growing between them.

"Do you like romance comedies? I think I could go for some perspicuous giggling," he chuckled more to himself as he coated the saucepan he planned to put the Spinach dip in.

"No thank you. I'm fine right here," and she shifted in the chair, gently turning another page.

The knocking stopped and the voices dissipated, now convened on the front lawn. Cliff could see through the blinds Merda standing in front of Mrs. Grant with her arms folded across her chest. He couldn't hear the conversation, but if he were to take a wild guess, Mrs. Grant, who looked every bit three quarters of a century; snorting out of wide nostrils, a wider mouth, and the widest hips on the block, was lecturing Merda on what she should do next.

"Devil be gone…" Cliff heard himself murmur.

Tebby heard him too. She looked up. "What did you say?"

He shook his head and went back to what he was doing…filling the saucepan with the Spinach dip he was preparing to bake. "Oh nothing," he sighed.

"Cliff, sometimes you be scaring me. Stop all that talking to yourself…" and she went back to reading, contradicting any signs of apprehension.

Closing the oven door and wiping his hands on a towel he walked over to her and stood in front of the chair. "Tebby, there are some mean people out here who really need to be taught a lesson. My sister is one of them. You may not see it…I don't think anyone but me actually sees it…but that's why I keep the door locked and try to avoid her." He paused, watching her watch him. "So, don't think I'm weird Miss Lady."

"I don't think you're weird Cliff. You're strange is all. You're not like most men."

That was a loaded thought. Where did he want to start? How should he tackle this loaded thought? "Haven't you ever wanted revenge on someone who's calculating and conniving, and consistently wishing you nothing but grief every waking step of your day?"

He didn't wait on her answer. "That's how it's been for me…" he dropped to his knees and stretched out on the floor. He loved what he had done to the ceiling, having it treated with a translucent coat that when he stared real hard, it looked like he was seeing through the ceiling to the sun.

"So, is that what this is about?"

He stopped mid-thought, actually taking pleasure in how right his life was going at the moment. So, he discarded the silly five-hundred a day pursuit. He found it wasn't money that would torment his arch tormentor anyway. It was his happiness, something he was dogged to shove in Merda's face. But Tebby's question sounded hostile, almost threatening.

"Is this what, what is about?" repeating the question.

She leaned over the chair, gleaming wildly, shoving the book in his face. "This!"

He crunched his face and squinted trying to read the text. He couldn't see a thing, except for the page she was on…page 194. But the book was about vampires and witches and celestial creatures that had nothing to do with this.

Tebby snatched the book out of his view and flipped back into the chair giggling hysterically. "Your plot here is waaaayyy too obvious," she laughed as loud as a docile miniature laugh could go. "I already know how this is going to end. Grejeckula is going to be sent to live out the rest of her life in Helveticas!"

Okay, so he learned from critics the story was a little thin. But how'd she guess he was writing about Merda? He didn't even realize this twist…until then. And this revealing finding, wholly accidental as it was, totally ruined the novel he was almost finished *cloaking*.

"So, I guess you're taking her side too?"

"Cliff, I'm not taking no one's side. I just think this would've been better if you'd switched things… making the witches come out as angels."

He lifted up, wanting to defend the book. But in that clip it dawned on him. She was right. Still, he didn't like it. It turned his stomach envisioning Merda as an angel.

CHAPTER ...6

Let it go! ...so said the Lord and every one of the Lord's pensive disciples. He knew he needed to let it go, but honest to goodness he couldn't. Whether others admitted it or not, but the mind overruled the heart, or was that the other way around?

The reason Tebby couldn't see his battle scars was because he never pulled each gritty tale out for her inspection. Sure he wrote most of this out, but he never told her in drivels each deed done; how Merda teased and whipped him at her pleasure. How she humiliated him in front of his girlfriends, the reason he stopped dating until she left home, and of course there was the church incident along with numerous daily happenings like the way she treated his childhood playmates.

He wanted to get these pictures out of his mind but just couldn't. For years he experienced nightmares over how she treated this one kid. The boy's name was Todd and Todd had just moved into the neighborhood. He came from a stock people called poor. And because everyone of color was of the underclass, this poor was subjective to simply being an outcast among the underclass. Todd lacked stylish clothes, was shy, and thus had no friends. So he buddied up with Todd, mostly because he felt bad for the guy always walking home alone.

One day as the both of them were walking home from school, Merda showed up, flanked as usual by some gangster-dressing thug with his arms hung around her, lusting over her body. Soon as he saw her turning the corner, his heart dropped. Fell between his knees and hit pavement. Whenever someone was with her, she was always her worst.

The thing about Todd, as he quickly learned, Todd was hard of hearing. Todd showed him the little piece he had to wear in his ear, which explained why every so often he had to keep repeating himself.

Just as they reached the part in the walk where Todd was to go one way and he the other, Merda caught up to them, looking out of those malicious beady eyes and giggling like her evil self. Snidely she scoffed, "what're you doing walking with this ragamuffin!?!"

Todd didn't hear her and continued walking. Cliff heard her clearly, but as he was accustomed to doing, he ignored her and continued walking home too. Later that night he told Mama what happened, also explaining how Todd was new to the neighborhood, his hearing impairment, and how none of the kids wanted to walk with him because his family was poor.

He wasn't sure which parts of what he told Mama affected her, but he'd never seen her more angry. For the first time since he could remember she really laid into Merda. She didn't hit her or anything, Merda was too big to be hit by then, but that night she really gave Merda an earful. It got so bad that his father had to intervene, of course taking Mama's side.

If he ever celebrated, it was that night, not knowing how short-lived the celebration was to be. Merda didn't let things go. She tormented him and Todd viciously after that, right up until the day the family moved. How someone could be so cruel and God be so forgiving was beyond his reasoning. He really wanted to get her out of his mind, but he just couldn't.

Kneeling on the bed beside Tebby he beamed wide, coming up with his greatest idea yet. "I know you're gonna frown when I say this, but I think I have an idea."

"Now whatcha' got gone on in that mind of yours?"

"I'm going to tell her I'm a spy," he said falling back on the bed, clasping his hands behind his head, gazing up at his amazing ceiling.

"A spy!?! A spy, Cliff? That woman is too smart to be believing you're some kind of spy."

She may have been that smart, but he wasn't done tormenting her. He still hadn't told Merda about losing his job. He went right from calling out sick to going on vacation. Thanksgiving was rounding the corner, so there would be time off for that occasion as well. Now he needed a nice stocky cushion for the time between then and now. A promotion and a transition fit perfectly. There would be time off and plenty of virtual work to do from home.

Tebby didn't care for it, but he loved the idea. The way it worked things out, he only had to string her along for a year. It would be enough time for her to tell as many nuances as she could gather, all the lies he'd been smearing her face in. Like the one unfamiliar legion she was cuing up to have him cremated, he guessed. "When people start acting erratically like this, it's either a signal of disease or death," he overheard her saying.

Mama was right. And idle mind indeed was the Devil's worshipping grounds, and he was going to play like an outlandish fool in the Devil's playground, just the way he pictured Tebby seeing him.

"Cliff, I just don't see why you don't march out there right at this moment and tell your sister…I lost my job, found another mouth to feed…so now bring it!"

He looked back at her, lying on the bed looking as straight-face as serious was sober, and chuckled, wryly however. *Bring it? Bring what*? He just wasn't a *bringing it* type of guy.

"Oh, I see, I have a little teaser here," and he tackled her in bed, making her giggle and squirm, twisting in the covers until he had her rolled up in a cocoon. "I've got you now," he laughed, tussling with her, though not sure what he wanted to do with her next. Instinctively he wanted to unravel her, and for the first time, make love to her. But up to this point he had been uneasy about touching her skin. Nearly two weeks had gone by and she had yet to clue him in that a more intimate relationship was suitable. A part of him wanted to quiz her on the matter, to find out what she may have been holding back, which happened to lead into the other part of his fear. Each time he looked at her he wanted to ask for legal documentation that would verify her birthdate. He hesitated to touch her otherwise.

But this time the toying and tussling became intense. He learned what aroused her the second morning of her being there after trying to wake her. Concerned by how difficult it was to rouse her, he casually remarked about how dangerous it must be for her living alone, sleeping as hard as she did.

"Not really," she shrugged, accompanied by a small laugh. "If you're sleep it doesn't really matter."

"Well, it matters to me," ready to ask if she, herself wasn't telling him everything he needed to know.

"The next time when that happens," ignoring his concern, and teasing like always, "blow on my neck. I hate air touching my neck. It goes down my spine and opens my eyes," she laughed.

The next morning, the same thing. He shook her, tickled her feet, whispered in her ear, and even dropped a book on the floor. Nothing. She did her little nuzzle, shifting positions, but wouldn't come out of the covers. Smiling, thinking about what she told him, he carefully lifted the covers and was about to blow on her neck when she sprang up, startling a little pee out of him.

But the third morning when he tried it, she really was knocked out. So he blew on her neck and to his surprise he had to turn away, pretending he hadn't seen anything. What he saw kept him locked in the bathroom for a good half an hour or more.

Between this anxiety he came up with many excuses. The state taking care of her meant she at least had to be emancipated. Her reasoning was sound, well beyond that which he considered objectionable culpability. And then there were her friends, like Naomi, or No-No, who lived in one of the larger hotels in Northeast who just about verified her age.

"Tebby," No-No started, aided by a Southern twang much like Tebby's, "I don't have it in me to be giving Deiga a bath today."

Godeiga was a tenant she and Tebby took turns looking after, giving her medicine, prepping her meals, bathing her and such. Godeiga weighed close to five-hundred pounds and couldn't do these things for herself. But Tebby and Naomi, who together soaking wet, didn't look more than a couple of hundred pounds, he couldn't see them managing all that weight either.

"Don't worry No-No. My friend will help me bathe Godeiga today."

The offer had his eyes fish-bowling around trying to imagine the project. What kind of special bathtub was this and how did they get a near five-hundred pound woman to get near it…forget putting her in it!?!

"Who?," No-No asked, peering around Tebby as if he wasn't standing right in front of her. But that was another thing about No-No. In addition to the missing teeth, and legs that no longer worked, she was partially blind, and was missing some of her hearing too.

"Me, Ms. Naomi," he bent over so that he wouldn't have to stretch his voice. "I'm Tebby's friend, Clifford."

No-No reared away. "Who?!? Clifford?"

"Yes No-No. This is my friend Cliff."

"Well, tell your Cliffy he don't need to be buzzin' in my ear. Sound like some kind of bee…bzzz…bzzz…buzzin' up my ear," she harked, abruptly looking back up at him. "Is that why they call you Stang?"

Clifford didn't know how to answer. He couldn't figure out where she got the name. She'd just called him by his real name? He looked over at Tebby, but when she shrugged, he made up an answer of his own. "Because my mama didn't like Sing," he played along.

No-No laughed a small rustic laugh, her little eyes igniting the dingy room, and swatted him on the knee. "How you know what ya' mama did and didn't like Stang? You was just a kid!"

"Cause she told me. She knew you was gonna one day come askin'."

"Stang, I thank you pullin' my leg now. You pullin' my leg, ain't you Stang?"

"Ms. Naomi, you ain't got no legs to pull."

"I do too have legs," and she hoisted her dress some to expose two pencil sticks sitting Indian style in the chair. "And why you callin' me Ms. Naomi like that? I ain't no Ms. Naomi to you. I'm just plain old No-No. I'm bout old as you anyway!"

"How old are you Ms. Naomi?"

"I told you I ain't no Ms. Naomi!"

"Okay… so then how old are you No-No?"

Naomi blushed, which chocolate as she was he could only tell by the way her eyes fluttered like butterflies that she just might have been around his age. "I'm fifty-nan," she answered on a bashful pretext.

Keeping the small surprise to himself, he smiled and found another distraction to occupy the conversation. In a corner of the room, opposite where he stood, was a stuffed animal. A happy stuffed grizzly bear he noticed when he first walked in. At first it looked like a lounge chair of some sort, except it was standing on its hind legs with its paws extended. But upon closer inspection the life size monster looked more real than he imagined.

He stared at the thing for a minute, trying to think of a reason why, out of all the lack of furnishings in No-No's place, she would keep such an odd knick-knack. It was much too large or, real looking, to call a stuffed teddy bear. Even if it indeed was furry and stuffed. It didn't quite fit the stature of modest décor, imposing as it was. The bear was about tall as him. Plus, a Buffalo Bills helmet sat on its head. Of all the worldly goods, non-perishables and perishables, why this eyesore?

"What 'chew thankin' on Mista Stang," reaching over and swatting at him again. "You fixin' on stealing my bear too Mister Stang?"

Struggle as he did, trying to stifle a laugh, he patted her hand. "Don't you worry ma'am...that bear will not be leaving this house...at least not with me."

"Ma'am!!!" she shrieked. "Awl, ain't no man old as you 'bout to be callin' me ma'am!" She looked over at Tebby walking in and out of the room gathering the things she needed to bathe Godeiga. "You hear your Cliffy in here callin' me these dirty names Teb?"

"No No-No, I didn't hear him. What's he callin' you?" And before she could answer, Tebby leaned over and pecked her on the jaw. "We've got to go now No-No. I left some fruit and cold-cuts in the frig, and will try to stop back by in a few days."

"Try!" Naomi shrieked again, leaving her duty of flirtatiously inspecting Cliff from head to toe. "So that's how you gonna do me...you find you a sweet ole' thang and then just turn your back on your No-No. Leave me in here with some old dried up fruit and some cold cuts I don't need to eat!"

Tebby ignored her though. "Just make sure you lock that top lock after we leave out," backing out of the door, bumping into him. "Don't pay her no mind. "She can be so sweet when she wants to be."

But he was paying No-No some mind, shrieking after them, "don't let that gal drown that pretty boy... have water splashing all down here drowning me too!"

"She's a little feisty thing, isn't she?"

"Is she," Tebby rolled her eyes. "She used to be a dancer for some exotic club and lost everything but that mouth...and her taste for men," Tebby said pushing the button that would take them up to the ninth floor, the floor where Godeiga lived.

"I kind of feel bad leaving her here like this," when what he really wanted to say was he felt bad taking Tebby away from her.

"Awl...she'll be okay. Trust me. No-No has plenty of friends around here. Sometimes I think she be passing secrets to Washington...everybody's place except hers has been robbed."

• • •

Visiting No-No was enough confirmation to assure him of Tebby's age without proof. And yet, he wasn't sure enough. The evidence had to be convincing. He wanted her to pull him on top of her, and then she had to wrap her arms and legs around him. Then he would be sure.

That's what brought him upright in bed, adding on to his greatest idea yet. "No, really…there's lots of secret service people around here," and he got cocky with the farce, "I'll tell her I'll have to kill her if she asks for details," gleaming wildly, hopelessly and haplessly in love with his new life. "She'll have to believe me!"

"Cliff, I don't know if I like the sound of this," and she unraveled the cocoon. "Why don't you tell her the truth? You can stay with me," she sulked as if she was growing bored with the silliness.

"How about I don't tell her the truth and you stay with me?"

One manly lesson his father left him with was that a man never asked for, nor accepted money in any form or fashion from a woman. Not ever. And for no reason. A man who supported his woman or family robbing banks was a better man than one who laid around the house milking money from a woman. They were the lowest beasts on earth his father said.

He could never live with Tebby, especially with her collecting SSI and disability. He already designated himself the sole provider. In fact, he didn't even want any SSI and disability funds associated with any address they ultimately would share. He would squirrel away every bit of savings he had left. And if that wasn't enough, he would sell the relics his father left behind, treasures Merda hadn't gotten her hands on because she had no idea there were paintings and a coin collection in the garage worth over $150,000.

Rolled up in a dusty rug were paintings his father brought back from Africa and tried to sell when he was a boy. He recalled the trip, and the heated arguments between his parents and a little spastic Jewish appraiser. His father thought the appraiser was cheating them. At first he valued the paintings at $50 each. But when his father decided to pay the man $50 for the appraisal and keep the paintings, the man suddenly discovered an error. The gallery offering to buy the paintings omitted a few zeros...by mistake. Fifty dollars turned into $5000 each. But his father no longer trusted the appraiser, or the gallery, igniting furious spats between him and his mother. Twenty thousand dollars wasn't chump change back then. Mama begged him to reconsider, which to squash the matter, his father trumped up a tale claiming the paintings had been stolen. The insurance company paid them $7000 for their loss, satisfying Mama, while the paintings stayed rolled up in a rug and stashed in the garage.

"Why don't you want to stay with me? You think your place is better than mine?"

"That's not it at all," and truthfully it wasn't. Though her place looked dimmer and seemed to hold more humidity than his place, he wouldn't have cared less about packing up and living with her, just for the sake of being with her. He could have stayed there and wouldn't have complained once about the dimpling mattress. Or the cold cement floors. Or the rectangular windows overlooking dumpsters that always smelled and seemed full. Or the clotheslines easily mistaken for electrical wires or telephone cables where clothes and shoes at all times hung. Or the uneven rooftops that had a look of tin cans peeled back. It wasn't material things he wholly cared about.

In face of the evidence, he wasn't a big spender, chasing fast women and cars, and buying flashy clothes type of guy. It was why he was out of a job, being satisfied in the position he had. It also was why Merda stayed on him. Preferring that he was the flashy get-rich getting over guy.

"She's not running me out of my home."

"So fine then...like I said...tell her '*I lost my job, found another mouth to feed, and so now bring it!*'"

They stayed quiet for a while, his head dancing around *bringing it*. Although Merda stopped calling him Satan didn't mean she wouldn't beat the Satan out of him if he tried to *bring it* like Satan. He would have to kill her for sure to keep from breaking another one of his father's rules. "*Never put your hands on a woman, son.*"

"You know Cliff," interrupting the *bring it* vision, "the more you want, the less you'll have."

Tebby was becoming too much Déjà vu. That was the same argument his father used for not selling the painting! They had a roof over their heads. Were eating three hot meals a day. So why sell his soul?

"I just want us to be able to enjoy this time we're having together," him now gazing up at his amazing ceiling. "I don't want to leave you for a second…"

"…But Cliff, we don't need no money to be secure."

She just didn't understand where he was going. And that's how it happened. He couldn't hold it a second longer. "Tebby, I love you," and his lips touched hers.

• • •

Making love to Tebby he couldn't' have imagined. He tried to, many nights tossing and turning on the couch, so tempted to slide in bed beside her, but nothing in those assaults compared to what followed after meeting her response with his lips.

She let her eyes shut and like cotton candy dissolves when touched by the tongue, she melted into his mouth and all but vanished without a trace.

Initially he was concerned about hurting her. It felt as if he was handling fine china, or porcelain, or an object just as easy to break. But when he looked into her face, and knew she was thinking what he was feeling, he closed his eyes too and enjoyed the fantasy.

Not that he had been able to focus much and write like his mind had been telling him he needed to, but after making love to Tebby he was in no shape to write at all. She bent his reasoning, smothered his thoughts, and stole his heart.

He couldn't deny it got beneath his skin, her going against how he should handle Merda, but then he'd have to disagree with what air meant to breathing to find fault with how important she was to him.

The arch in her back made her stretch appear more graceful. He traced the curve with his eyes when she reached up to run her hands through her hair. It wasn't the long mane most women preferred. She wore her hair in a style similar to Merda's, except without the gel and lotions that gave her more of an authentic Native look.

"Cliff, I'm not coming back here if you don't do the right thing with that sister of yours," she said rubbing her eyes.

What!?! He pulled up to his knees, to kneel behind her. "Are you telling me that after making such amazing love you could leave out of here like that?"

She turned around to face him, looking every bit Tebby…flattering and alluring. But somehow she looked wiser and older too. Perhaps it was the tears filling her eyes. "I've had enough trouble in my life. I just don't want any more."

"That's why I'm doing this Teb," and he shushed her tears pelting her forehead with kisses. "Please don't leave me with this choice," and he felt the tears coming to his defense as well. "Please Teb, don't do this to us."

He pushed back knowing what he had to do. "I'll make Grejeckula a sister, and don't think I won't, if you think of leaving me," he teased.

It almost did the trick. She smiled and buried her eyes in his hands. "I'm serious Cliff," she sang, "we have enough to take care of ourselves and make bills without having to stay here."

"That may be, but my father taught me never to live off no woman."

"Well, did your father say anything about doing honest work? Spying don't sound so honest to me."

"But I won't be really spying." Why couldn't she see this? "I'll be…" and he lost his place. Somewhere along the way the argument took a left turn, confusing him. *What would he really be doing*? *Why was he lying*? And then it came back to him. Merda! Nothing would be right until he could get back the spirit she'd stolen from him.

"Cliff, money and things don't do nothing but kill the spirit and dreams."

He caught her by the shirttail as she rose up off the bed. It was a few days before Thanksgiving and she was headed over to No-No's where they made dinners around this time for those unable to cook.

"Where are you going? Come back here, I'm not finished with you yet," he laughed, pulling her back into him.

"Oh yes you are Cliff. You go in there with that spy lie and you most certainly will be finished with me!"

• • •

The giggling Tebby was gone. She wanted him to throw in the towel, move out, and move in with her. But he couldn't see it, for more reasons than following his father's leading piece of advice. The things Tebby did for others who couldn't do for themselves was great, and call him a hypocrite too, but the beggar role was only a skit. He'd have to be unconscious and seriously delirious too, deliberately living out such a skit.

But he couldn't just like that, walk away from it all. He spent thousands of dollars turning one room into an efficiency Better Homes might love to snap a photo of and place among their collection. And despite the nosey neighbors, he also loved the area. It attracted the best side of sunlight during the summer. Welcomed the fall colors without grief. Provided an awesome winter wonderland view. And spring, believe it or not, the neighborhood birds actually lined up on his window sill and sang to him.

So no! He couldn't back down. Well, maybe not to Merda. Tebby was different.

He went right *in there* with the spy lie. It happened as matter-of-factly as how he ended up making love to Tebby. He teetered up to the front door meeting Merda blocking his path after dropping Tebby off. At first, pretending he hadn't noticed her standing there filling the entire doorframe, with his head down he swept one foot over a patch of dirt that had blown onto the sidewalk. Of course he was buying time. He had taken to heart what he and Tebby talked about. They had only known each other a few weeks, but in those three weeks it felt as if they had been together three decades. He didn't want to lose her, and certainly not over a spy lie.

This was the funny thing, him also stooping over to examine a rose bush by steps. Out of all the years that rosebush had been there, and probably patch of dirt too, he never once paid either one iota of attention. Now, in a hollow reckless moment, there he stood examining a rosebush for prosperity and good health.

"Oh, hey…I didn't see you standing there," he said adding a phony show of surprise when he looked up and saw Merda standing there, arms folded across her chest, face twitching, glaring, murderously mad.

"Clifford Blanchard…" she spat as he eased by, "I never thought I'd live to see the day you acting so like you've lost your mind!"

Because he'd already passed her, she followed on his heels, breathing down his neck. "Do you have any idea what this is doing to Mama and Dada?"

He tried hastening his step in the direction of his room. If he could move quickly enough, he might make it before one of her torts hit him so hard in the back he would be forced to turn around and address her back.

"You lying up in there with that young girl," and she put special notes on *young girl*, making it sound as if Tebby was two,"…like you don't have no good common sense. It's gonna cost ya! It's going to cost you big time brotha!" And she wasn't calling him brotha' in no kind of affectionate way either.

He had almost gotten by Parker, when one step past the laser that lined up the remote resting in Parker's lap perfectly with the television, she herald over his back, "And brotha, if you think I'm gonna let some white broad take all Mama and Dada slaved for, you got another thought coming!"

White broad!?! That was one he never suspected to be coming. "Merda, she is as black as you and I! And since when did Christians start talking like racists?"

Maybe he was colorblind, but in case he wasn't, then Tebby wasn't much fairer in complexion than either of them. Tebby, in fact, had more honey in her sauce than the loafer stuffed in his mother's lounge chair.

The room was dark, save for the flashes of light coming from the television, so he couldn't make out much of Merda's face with her partly hidden by a shadow. The most he could make out was the white of her eyes spilling over her pupils. Reminded him of the Damned Children from the seventies Damned movie.

"I'm no racist," she spat. "And don't you dare try to turn my words into a holy war! Just you wait! Let her get tired of you and she'll run right down to that precinct with her lily-white looks and turn your old simple behind in for rape! Then tell me who's the racist!"

If a calendar had been nearby he would have checked it for the year. "So what if she does? Do you think it hurts more if a white woman beats me down to dust, than a black woman shooting me in the dirt?"

She couldn't answer. She wanted to. She even tried to. But she had no words to.

"…Besides, I'm protecting that woman. She's in a witness protection program," he blurted.

That one line did it. It did the trick. Sealed the deal. And the thing about it was, it came out so naturally. All the tapioca was there. His head swinging low. Sloped shoulders. And the pity he parcel post and obligingly hand delivered over to Merda, smeared all across her face like jam over bread.

Took the wind right out of her sail. One minute she was up, the angel of righteousness and all things good, and the next…well the next thing he knew, her pupils gradually grew back. She fell face first flat into the spy novel, ignoring Parker's concentrated look lining up the remote with the TV's radar.

Parker, he could tell, wasn't buying it, not with the scrupulous effort he was putting into changing channels. It reminded him of the look Hagerstown had given him. *You lying bastard. Save your worthless soul and shut up now.*

But then why would Merda have known to look back at Parker for reassurance? The man knew nothing about national or federal security work. He hadn't held a job since quitting high-school.

By the time he finally made it to his room, after douching Merda with every bit of mustard left in his jug, a black coat twice the duty of wearing a burqa fell over him. What was he thinking? The sense of dread was so heavy that he was positive in that given moment he would murder Merda if he lost Tebby over this.

CHAPTER...7

The Spy. That's who he now was. He didn't have to toil too long trying to remember what he told Merda. True to her character she called everyone. Verizon had to be opening her own billing department for all the calls she placed and people she told. He imagined how the conversation went, something like the way it did when he almost walked in on her church committee meeting. He was almost to the entranceway when he heard her, "sssh...don't let this get out."

He stopped on the dime. If he rounded the corner and showed his face she would have stopped talking, and he wanted to hear. It could have been something about him, or better, her.

"You know why Pearl put her daughter out?"

One of the committee members tried to answer but got it wrong. She was reciting the g-rated censored *for publication* version. He stretched his ear around the corner to get the untainted x-rated version. The version Merda whispered, though she really didn't have to. There was no one in the house but the women she was telling the secret to, all with mouths bigger than hers.

It took a minute but he finally caught on to the implication, "…she caught her in her room with another girl." By evening that same day, the secret was no longer a secret. Everyone who knew anyone that attended the scholarship meeting knew to shun Pearl's daughter.

Surely it was the same way she handled his secret, despite the abject repercussions that she could be killed if she opened her mouth. Just one more person who couldn't keep their mouth shut to save their life.

He hurried by the women to his room. Didn't even give them a chance for a good hand wave greeting. Already it was all over town that he had been shacking up with a young girl. Most suspected it was a young runaway, likely in her late teens, but it still didn't sit well with those who thought a fifty-two year old man should behave better. But then too, this was Cliff they were talking about. The man who at fifty-two had never married, had no children, and still lived in his parent's house. He wasn't right to begin with. Plus he was a writer. It all fit, and came together even better now that he was a spy.

Of course not everyone believed this. Not everyone was as gullible as Merda. Those who knew better, like those with husband's or even they themselves, who worked in Bethesda and D.C. and Arlington, knew this didn't sound right. No one in their right mind walked around calling themselves a spy. But those who knew better also knew enough not to address the matter with Merda. In an egregious way it made the buzz more satisfying. People laughing in Merda's face behind her back seemed so fair.

That evening however, and the next day when mostly family and close church friends were over, the tables started to turn. Government people who know the business refrained from any work-related comments during socials, but it wasn't the case for those working in places where Merda and Parker frequented…AIDE Centers, the couch, the kitchen, and bed.

Every last one of them walked in the door, knew he was a spy, and wanted to hear down to the last spy note everything there was to know about the spy business. She invited at least fifty people over for dinner, so he was telling the story fifty times, sometimes likely, in fifty different ways.

Theresa was first. She walked right in while the greens were still being chopped and dropped into pots, and could tell there was something *new* about him. Actually there wasn't too much of anything that got by Theresa. She knew people very well…too well…even people she didn't know well at all.

Like Bin Laden…she knew more about what that man was thinking and planning than probably Bin Laden himself. McNabb was another one. She knew what he wanted to say but didn't say to the press who interviewed him about his going to Washington. Name anyone, say anything, and she knew who had been sleeping beneath people's beds and living in their business. Nothing got by her. She had this thinking ahead, sort of like ESP. The one thing she didn't know, otherwise she wouldn't have been smiling as much, was how annoying he found it seeing her mouth peeled back so far when she was missing so many teeth. Five or six teeth were up there in the front, but none in the back. How could someone with as many missing teeth find the nerve to laugh about at anything, much less at anyone else. But this was Theresa.

"So tell me a secret Cliff," and there she was in his face grinning the naked gums hanging on to a few teeth.

"I don't know any secrets," he answered turning away, losing his appetite for the day.

"Not even an itty-bitty secret?" And here's the real kicker, not that it lends heavily to much of anything, but Theresa was married to a man who just retired from the CIA. Alvin…or 'ole Al behind his back…a white man. The thing about 'ole Al was also behind his back it was rumored he had ties with the Klu Klux Klan. Yep, the good 'ole KKK, and Theresa, with her brown skin and naked grinning gums didn't suspect this, or at least she didn't let on she believed this. No, when Theresa wasn't grinning in everyone else's business, she was busy ranting about why Obama needed to be in office, which was something else she didn't know that everyone else suspected. 'Ole Al was a staunch Republican. How's that for how much Theresa knew?

Otherwise, Theresa was an alright woman. Aside from Merda, she was one of his first sitters. She got him his first real date…for the prom. And his first real drink, and cigarette, and reefer, and 'head job' too…friendship stuff. So when he said he liked Theresa and thought she was alright, he really meant it. She hadn't done half the things Merda had done to him. In fact, she often looked over him, protecting him from even Merda.

"No, Terry…not even an itty-bitty secret," he glumly muttered again, pulling off the apron and tossing it over the back of a chair. Those two could go on cackling and finish preparing the dinner because he was done.

"Now where ya' going Inspector Gadget," Theresa ribbed, "you know before the night is over I'm going to get a secret out of you!"

And she lived up to her promise, working him hard. They all did. After Theresa, a round woman walked up to him, a woman who he hadn't recalled seeing before but soon learned she was Mrs. Grant's *baby* daughter. The round woman plopped on the couch next to him, grinning evocatively with a plate perilously close to spilling over balanced on her stomach. She wanted to know how she could get a job, "where he worked at."

"Who are you," he asked returning her mannerisms.

She leaned away. "You don't remember me? I'm Carrie's daughter!"

She really wasn't supposed to answer that. Even if he didn't happen to remember the smaller chunky face coming up for its final gasp of air out of the larger face.

He lost more of his appetite looking in her plate. Some people took time placing food on their plates, trying to avoid keeping certain foods from touching. Not her. It was difficult to tell what was burying what. It just looked like a large colorful mountain on her plate.

"Yeah Cliff, how much they pay for that kind of work anyway!?!" Squealed another woman standing parallel to Mrs. Grant's baby daughter.

"Me and a friend of mine just went in to take the test to be a guard at the CIA…they was talkin' about starting us…if we pass the test, at forty-five."

There, that was the right word. *If.* Even *if* she passed every written, oral, and psychological test given, there was no way she was passing the physical…not with all that gumbo around her waist.

Normally he didn't berate large women. After all, he had rounded off over the years, plus, one of the largest women there had to be his Aunt Idell, whose ample cushion only made her more lovable. The others, many he assumed were neighbors or church family, could ride off into a deep dark sunset and, as large as they were, he'd never miss one of them. He never went to church, and other than an occasional wave across the street to a figure he only waved at because it waved at him first, he never said two words to these people. As the neighbors he knew died off and their children grew up…and out, and he started splitting 99% of his time between the office and his bedroom, neighbors became strangers. Often he didn't even recognize the neighborhood.

The anger festering inside him he soon realized grew from this familiar niggerish jaw-breaking crowding him in. The forty-five *thou* number blossomed and swelled into an ungodly awful figure.

A chocolate girl standing near the CIA possible had better information. Her brother was a SPO. *They* started him at seventy-five, and now he was about to retire… "yep, he been there over…umm…" she looked up at the ceiling counting back, eyelashes flickering and fluttering as she counted, "…umm…over thirty years now," she rattled, tearing a piece of ham apart with her greasy fingers and throwing it to the back of her mouth.

The thing was, the chocolate girl wasn't fat at all. Her hair was a little peppery, knotted up on her head as if no one would look past the two scoops of chiseled jello shaking behind her hips, but she wasn't fat. So why was he looking her up and down, seething inside about her boxed toes she bunched into a pair of pointy-toe shoes.

"If you make it in, you got to be able to swim," so says the chocolate girl.

Please, muscle mama would sink like a rock, he grimly thought as another taller and older woman leaned into the dialogue.

"My daughter is a SPO. She didn't have to know how to swim," raised the older woman matching every word to a fantastic beat of the most wickedly flapping eyelashes he'd ever seen. These lashes were about three inches long, and very, very dark and thick. Altogether he'd say they weighed a couple of pounds each. So each word she said, and he counted about ten so far, one lash would go up and then down, followed by the other. They didn't flutter at the same time, which was good considering how stuffy it was getting in the corner.

And that's when it happened. Jamison, baby brother of his mother, and one of the more colorful in the family, barged between the ladies resting his chin on the chocolate girl's shoulder. "So Cliffy, where's this sweet young thang I hear you been back there shackin' with?"

Any other day he would have let Jamison slide with this type of question. But trapped in a corner, hot, irate, and most annoyed by Jamison's greasy look too, things went further than he would have liked.

First off, he and Jamison had this love-hate thing going on. He loved Jamison when he was penning his colorful antics to the characters in his stories, but hated being in his company. For one, he had one of those juicy mouths. When he talked, because he was missing a few side and bottom front teeth, coupled by a drinking problem, he spat…a lot.

At the point of explosion, though no one would know it by how coolly he told Jamison he wasn't shacking up, he could feel himself rising above them all, about to pull out and bring together a large tambourine, once and for all.

"He ain't shacking," the chocolate girl leaned away to inform Jamison.

"Yeah, he a spy," Mrs. Grant's baby daughter argued in a giggle.

"Okay…okay…so then if you a spy, then what's the code?" Jamison drooled on the chocolate girl's shoulder.

Enough. If Jamison thought he was a comedian, then he had a really short memory. It wasn't long ago, as he was sharing time with mopping floors, cleaning toilet bowls and emptying trash cans for companies that never invited his kind to their Christmas parties, he would have recalled that stand-up comedy stint where he blew up the stage. He was so bad, loving his poop and fart jokes so much that the club owner pulled the plug on his act, embarrassing all of them who had come to hear him cut up, as it turned out, on Parker.

He stayed on Parker, asking when was the last time he got out of the chair, betting he hadn't washed in weeks, sniffing in the air to insinuate he hadn't brushed his teeth either. He wasn't even marginally funny, laughing at his own jokes and having the nerve to ask the audience if they got it? Hell yeah, they got it. But did he get it?

You're a janitor Jamison! A clean-up man working in one of the stinkiest fields a person can have. Here's twenty sticks of gum for you. The stuff coming out your mouth stinks!

Hanging on for dear life on the tip of his tongue he was about to end the night telling them all he was in love with Tebby. Fine, he made up his mind. He would pack up his things and be out by morning. This secret service skit wasn't working. If he really were involved with secret work, he'd be in serious trouble. Big serious trouble. And so might they. But what he wanted to say never got airborne.

The words never even got to taxi down the runway, or push back from the terminal for that matter. They just hung on the tip of his tongue as his old favorite Aunt Idell crept between the huddle, rocking from side to side and panting, swatting at Jamison just before easing onto the sofa beside him.

"Ah," she wheezed after the worth of her weight sank into the sofa. "Go on with ya'lls nonsense. I just want to sit beside my nephew for a while," she smiled, patting his leg.

Cliff smiled too. Who wouldn't want an Aunt Idell taking their side? The slither of turkey he held up slid across his tongue nicely. Not only was she the right kind of warm and cuddly, her voice carried an edge that would cut to a bloody carnage anyone who dared to irk him. Someone could be talking about eggs, and it be upsetting his stomach, and she would shut down whoever was talking about eggs. That was Aunt Idell.

"Nan, Cliffy finally got him a sweet young thang he been keepin' up in here tryin' to have us believin' he protecting her! Yeah right. Tell the truth...how much work you be gettin' done at night," Jamison teased.

Two things. Jamison was everything and then some, but one thing he wasn't, and that was a fool. Even if he didn't know, he knew. That's because he never talked from his head, but spoke from his heart. And one thing the heart never did, and that was lie, which brought him to the matter of the other thing. For thirty minutes he'd been aching to make his peace and call it a night. But each time he tried to push back, someone would cut him off. He could be mistaken, since he never attended church, but it felt like God's hand trying to cover his mouth. Well, after what transpired, transpired, he was sure it wasn't the case, but then again, who really knew?

All he heard was, "*Sex, sex, sex! That's all that's on the brain nowadays!*" Followed up by charming old Aunt Idell, "and yeah, murder, murder, murder, and crime, crime, crime! Ain't you sick of hearing that mess too? Killin' up our kids and homes... But I guess not, since the Bible you read all day seems to think it's okay!"

And man, did this not wipe out the night. Shut it down...D-O-double u-N! Don't ask who was saying what, and which line belonged to whom, because after it was said and done, he was ready to run.

"How can you say such an evil thing? God is—"

"—Evil!?! Evil brought your tail in this world!"

Gasp! And there stormed off the fan.

"You big fat bitch, don't be talkin' to my ainty like that!"

"Whoa…whoa…" and that was Jamison. He did step in. "Ain't gonna be none of dat!"

Jamison did all he could, but then Theresa and Merda and a few other able-bodied women joined the mêlée. Again, don't ask who was saying what, and which line belonged to whom, because other than Aunt Idell and Jamison, it was hard to tell.

"We need prayer in this house right now!"

"No! What we need in here is some truth…this one got they hand in the collection plate… the other one in the pastor's lap…and that one over there ain't doin' no betta than any of us!" Of course that was Aunt Idell, Mother of No Mercy. She lived the best years of her life. She was now free to speak her mind.

"She goin straight to hell! Straight to hell! I ain't hanging around here. I got to get out of here!"

"Well go! Git! Go on out there and take the rest of the Pastor's drug money out the vault!" Aunt Idell was tickled hot. Laughed loud, she was on a happy roll.

"Idell, stop it! You stop it rig—"

"—Drug money? What's she—"

"—No! Let her fat ass talk. Karma's coming for her!"

"Hey, hey, what I say about talkin' like that—"

"—awl Jamison, you need to sit down. I bet it was you who got all this mess started anyway!"

"But how you gonna let her sit over there calling our pastor a drug lord?"

"Pastor know all that money in the collection plate ain't clean money. His hands dirty too."

"Oh Lord, where's my coat…and my purse? I got to get out of here!"

"And you go on too," Aunt Idell chuckled. "But you best first call your husband before you go in there."

A small dark object shot across the room, coming fast in their direction. His and Aunt Idell's. It was small and fleeting enough to be a bird, but outweighed any small bird he knew of, going through the window the way it did. He moved just in time, shielding Aunt Idell to keep her out of harms way, too.

Scuffling ensued, and tussling, grunting and some more cursing, but nothing he could see wrapped around Aunt Idell the way he was. When it was over and the smoke cleared, one card table leaned on two legs. The contents once on the table all slid to the floor. A picture hung on the wall…lopsided. The dinning table, once beautifully dressed with candles and much of his mother's fine crystal and china, looked like a heap of mismatched food and broken glass.

Shaken and distraught, Merda hadn't heard what precipitated the exchange, but blamed him anyway. "How could you have let this happen," she sobbed. "This totally ruined dinner."

He wouldn't have dare uttered it, though he sure was thinking it. *There's always next year.* Maybe next time she might not invite so many hostile Christians. *Weren't they supposed to be loving and patient? Letting no matter what came out of Aunt Idell's mouth, roll off their backs?* No, they couldn't. Apparently the truth really hurt. Only lies and cover-ups pacified and healed believers. Exactly why he wasn't ready to tell the Merda the truth.

In all fairness, Pastor Edmonds was a good man. Despite Aunt Idell's harsh accusations, his hands were clean, his heart was clean, and so was his mission. At least that's what he took from the man. Not even Aunt Idell's contemptuous accusations tainted this fact. Let the record speak for itself, he had been with Tabernacle for twenty-five years, and saved quadruple the souls. When the church roof was blown off during a bad storm and there was no place to worship the Sunday after, he opened his home, and would have continued doing so until a temporary place to worship was found.

So he wasn't in agreement at all with what Aunt Idell was saying. What he enjoyed was Aunt Idell getting the attention off the spy. Even as Merda ranted, sobbing and picking up broken glass, the spy was the last thing on her mind. Oh, he was on her mind. Just not the spy.

• • •

None of it was his fault, though she blamed him anyway. He shouldn't have gotten Jamison worked up. He knew how *he* was. And he should have stopped Aunt Idell. He knew how *she* was too. The cobwebs in his head causing him to chase *in behind* that young tail was what caused Mama's dishes to be broken and her memories now all gone.

He could see she was upset and talking from grief. Wasn't no point arguing back, not with the defense he had in mind. Mama was more than those broken dishes. In fact, he wished the dishes were dead instead of Mama. And she knew how Jamison and Aunt Idell was too. She shouldn't have invited them. And to settle all matters, he told her he'd have to kill her if she told anyone about his spy work. But did she listen? No, she told everyone still, which had nothing to do with what really got Jamison going. Her blabbing her trap about him seeing Tebby and robbing a cradle got Jamison going. It was all her fault. Every bit of it. And no he wasn't replacing the broken dishes.

"Cliff, before you leave out of here I hope you understand that woman is not welcome here."

This had to be why God covered his mouth. Tebby was right, he needed to stand up to Merda and put her in her place once and for all. For too long he overlooked her, ignored her, excused her, avoided her…it was time to now stand up to her.

"You may not care or have forgotten, but this is my house too, and my career, so I can care less about what you think, care, want, or feel."

Her reaction wasn't expected. Merda could be an Aunt Idell replica if provoked. She didn't go around raising her voice and fighting people, at least not any more, but there had been times when she would lose it and basically act like a nut. With Mama's broken dishes and Thanksgiving down the toilet, he waited on this reaction. He even had his hand on the doorknob, preparing to bolt out the door, yes, like a chump.

"But we live here together…" she pleaded. "You have to be respectful of everyone in here…not just you Clifford Blanchard," she snarled, angrily enunciating the ss's in the hiss when there were no ss's in his name.

"How would you like it if I brought a gang member in here to live with us…" and she grabbed extra ammo, "…what if the gang member was the person after that woman." The look in her eyes turned from a plea to glee.

She knew she had him. "See...see how we have to respect our home? You should have never accepted that assignment without first talking to me."

Okay, so she had a point, but only if Tebby had really been in a witness protection program. But there was no witness, and there was no protection program. So Merda could go on and invite all the gang-bangers she could scrounge up. She was the only one who didn't have a deadbolt on her bedroom door.

"You're right," the boom in his voice never ceasing to amaze him, "I should have never told you about this assignment. But because I did, look at the mess you started."

The Green Mile was the first thing that came to mind as he watched her complete her transformation. She easily took care of the Black National Flag, turning from brown to Black to red and then yellow. Add in the orange and green, and white for her eyeballs and she made it through every color of the rainbow.

"How dare you blame that disaster on me! I worked on that dinner all week brotha...while you were—"

"—and that's your problem," he cut her off, none too interested in hearing how many potatoes she peeled or onions she cried over. "If you cared as much about my work as you do yours, you would have kept your big trap shut!"

He couldn't go straight to Tebby's place telling her how terrible Thanksgiving had gone after she told him not to go in there with the spy lie. He had to drive around and come up with a plan to clean up the mess he made.

Bringing Tebby right back might cause another scene, but he didn't want to spend another night without her. He might get away with spending the day out and about with her, and then sneaking her in after Merda had gone to sleep, but how long might that take. Sometimes Merda would be in her room, awake and reading, until one-two in the morning. Tebby might get suspicious.

Perhaps he could make up an excuse to spend the weekend with Tebby…until Sunday when Merda was sure to be in church. This Sunday she might be in there longer than other Sundays given how tragic things turned out. But then he didn't bring a change of clothes.

The further he drove, the angrier he got. Why should he be the one sneaking around? *But then, oh that's right, he was the one who put the lie out there*. Still, Merda had a bad habit of doing whatever she pleased, and then finding a precious scripture that forgave her. She had no inclination some things weren't forgivable.

He found Roscoe still under the awning selling those fake precious stones, only this time along with a new hot deal; lithographs pressed on t-shirts. Why he went to see Roscoe could only be explained as desperation. He could have never brought himself to seriously harm his sister. He severely disliked her, but not enough to ruin his chances of never seeing Tebby again. When he thought of Roscoe, he was thinking about creating a rumor that would teach Merda about spreading rumors. She needed business to be concerned about, to keep her off his back.

From a distance he made Roscoe out by his hunched over bulky figure stuffed in the long black wool coat he wore beneath a fatigue jacket.

"Hey Rosc my man," he greeted him from behind.

Roscoe spun around. He didn't recognize him at first, and probably not even after greeting him, but being the entrepreneur he was, he greeted him warmly. "My friend, how have you been," reaching out and clutching his hand by two scratchy wool gloves with the fingers poking out. "So, I see you ran into some new money," standing back to check him out, clean shaven, sheepskin Shearling coat, matching hat, and cashmere scarf draped around his neck.

"All man, it's nothing," not feeling as comfortable as he would've liked, shrugging off the compliment with a blasé smile. "Just tryin' to stay warm."

"And it looks like you're doing a good job. —Hey, I need you to come look at something for me," wasting no time, doing that old familiar bounce to the other end of the table. "Got some new pieces in…flown in last week."

Cliff looked down. The table was filled with much of the same things he remembered from his last visit. He started to admire another bangle, but recalled how the last bracelet didn't make it to the coffee shop where he met Tebby. Looked down and the bangle was gone.

"Psst…psst…" he heard. "Down here."

He looked beneath the table at a cardboard box that made him laugh when he saw what was in the box. Framed velvet pictures. Of black men and women. Mostly women. And most nude. Either the top, bottom, or both. Provocative paintings, but erotic and beautiful. An image he'd love to see done of Tebby one day.

"Man! Where'd you find these," juicing up his voice. As beautiful as the pictures were, taking him way back, he wasn't interested, unless there was one of Tebby.

"I can take it out the frame…you roll it up…reframe it any way you like…" he laughed, showing his teeth. He must not have paid it any attention before, but this time he noted the spaces between each tooth…top and bottom. Roscoe's smile kind of reminded him of a piano, and something his grandmother used to tell them. "You shouldn't trust a person with gaps between their teeth.

One gap," she said, "was a person with great wisdom. But more than one gap was the work of the devil."

"Say Rosc man," since they seemed to be hitting it off alright, "Do you know where I can find some…" and rather than say it, he demonstrated, bringing his hand to his mouth like how he remembered seeing Jamison do it when he was looking for weed.

Roscoe looked at him, hard, as if his intentions could be read through his eyes. "Say my friend, this is all Rosc got here," and he dropped the cloth and started dusting over his wares, straightening them up and brushing over them as well.

"Hey Rosc man, it's me…remember…you got me for fifteen last time. I know I don't look like I did the last time, but I'm not the police."

Roscoe turned around, not losing one stride in his skit, "for you my man, let me show you these silk ties I brought back just cause I knew you was stoppin' by."

At first Cliff thought Roscoe was going to go on ignoring him. He even started to walk away, but Roscoe caught him by the arm. "Hey, hey where you going my friend. Rosc got something here for er'one."

He pressed the fattest and ugliest necktie he'd ever seen in his hands. "Go on…look at it," Roscoe gleamed. "For you, that's only sixty-f-a-v-e dollas'…" he laughed hustler style.

It took a minute to catch on, before he happened to see the tag hanging onto the garment. He looked up, wanting to ask if he at least had a prettier tie but thought not to push the envelope. "You accept credit?"

"Oh course I do my friend. Right this way." He swiped the credit card and continued with the skit. "My friend, when you put on this tie and er'body see you in it…my friend…you, and er'body lookin' at you, gonna think you flying!"

• • •

"Cliff, I can't lie to no man wearing a collar."

"Okay…so I'll tell him to dress casual."

She laughed, though the look on her face was dead serious. "I told you not to go in there with that lie in the first place."

He told her a part of the story, leaving off everything but the part where Pastor Edmonds wanted to meet with them. He wouldn't have been able to stand looking Tebby in the face, explaining how awful things turned out. It may have not been a big deal to her, but at the moment it was tearing him apart knowing why he really wanted to stay with her for a few days.

"Have I ever told you how pretty you are? You are the most beautiful woman I've ever seen."

"Cliff," she sighed, "I don't care what you say. You're not going to get me to tell a lie to that man."

"What if you let me do all the talking…I'll tell him you're mute or something."

"Cliff, what is wrong with you? That man will know I'm not a mute!"

"How?"

"Because I'll be talking!"

"I just can't loose you Tebby…I just can't…"

"Have you done any writing while I was gone?"

No he hadn't. Between missing her and dealing with Merda and Thanksgiving, how could he? But to answer her question, "I've started working on another piece."

"Another piece? But I liked the other one you were working on."

Yes, he'd come up with another piece. It was a piece he'd been fumbling around with in his mind. *Turning the Other Cheek*. It was another cheeky paranormal story. A lot of characters were going to be turning the other cheek, only these were going to deserve it. But it was a little too soon to lay it all out for Tebby. He left it at, "it wouldn't fit into the one they were working on."

"Cliff, where are you taking me?"

"Out."

"Out where?"

"Out to eat."

"But why? I thought your sister and her friend were making all this food and were going to have so much left over. You mean, you guys ate it all?"

Could he feel any worse? "No, I just want to see what you look like beneath a chandelier." He glanced over at her, looking straight ahead with a small smile on her face. Just the sweetest image. She was a mirage of what every goddess was meant to look like. Books all described them like beauties, but he saw those early BC drawings and they weren't so beautiful to him. Tebby was like an imaginary cloud made into the shape of a woman. Obscure, but real.

"So, how's No-No and them doing?"

"Just fine. We fed over 7000 people you know."

No, he didn't know, feeling even worse. Even if the ending to their Thanksgiving hadn't ended as tragic they still wouldn't have come close to that number.

"Well, I guess leftovers are out over at your place too, huh?"

• • •

He lay affably still on Tebby's frail mattress staring up a waterlogged ceiling. Everything that could be wrong with the apartment was wrong. Not enough electrical outlets. Drafty windows. Rusty plumbing. Dry-rotted wood, creaky floors, and too, the frail mattress. But they made good use of their time together. Staring up at the ceiling he thought about the past twenty-four hours; laughing through dinner, writing sections of the novel on napkins, and taking in a comedy show where they laughed the rest of the night away at two comedians who they couldn't remember one bit of either routine.

Got back to Tebby's place, tipsy…very tipsy, and passed out in each others arms. He woke up and found Tebby curled up beside him, tucked in like a little kitten, and him staring up at the ceiling thinking about all the improvements he could have done to spruce up the place. Well that, and a few other things.

As usual she didn't budge. Throughout the squeaky faucet he turned on and off, and the creaky noises he made walking to the adjacent room, which really wasn't a separate room, it was more like the space over, she slept through it all.

In a drafty corner he called the Youth Center where Merda worked one day a week—Fridays. It was a job linked through the church. When she was playing Mrs. Big Shot she talked as if she was running things; having to open up, or do the books, or narrating a lengthy exchange she had with a parent who didn't know how to take care of their child. She didn't fool him. He knew exactly who ran the Center. He asked to speak to Cathy.

"This is Cathy," a chirpy voice unexpectedly purred in his ear. It was Saturday. He had hoped a careless employee answered the phone. That's who he wanted to leave his message with. But it was Cathy who answered, so he closed his eyes and recited a quick prayer. *If Merda could be forgiven for all the grief and pain she caused him, then so might he.*

"Ugh…yes, hi Cathy…" and he got right to the core of the issue. In summary he had a neighbor who he believed was using drugs. He knew she worked around children and thought she should be tested.

Cathy seemed surprised. She asked him to repeat the name of the employee a few times. It sounded highly unusual for this particular employee, but she agreed with him, no harm could come by requesting she take the test. But she wanted to know more about him. How did he know *this* employee, other than living down the street as he put it? And why her? Why hadn't he contacted child protective services if he had concerns about her being around his grandchild? She appreciated the call but couldn't help but be a little suspicious. In twenty years of operation she never received a call as bizarre, and certainly never expected to receive a call on this particular employee.

Satisfied he ended the call and waited for Tebby to awake. While he waited, he paced, his heart sinking each time he retraced his steps. *An eye for an eye left the whole world blind.* His mother quoted that one all the time. It still wasn't too late to back out.

Back and forth, from the window to about the center of the room he paced. It was just a call he kept telling himself...until a cramp caught him around the heart. He hoped Cathy hadn't been smart enough to jot down his number, or worse, and his heart raced when he thought about it. His cell phone number could be stored on her caller ID. One look at the number and...he chose not to think about it. Besides, if Cathy called Merda in for a testing right at that moment, she would test fine. And if call was traced back to him, he'd just have to say he lost his cell phone, and of course buy a new one.

"Who were you talking to," Tebby whispered so softly he thought he was hearing things. Spinning on his heels it startled him to see her standing there.

"How long have you been up...I—I thought you were still sleep."

CHAPTER...8

He walked in the house and right by Parker, hand in hand with Tebby trailing behind. It was Sunday, Merda was in church, likely praying for someone who wished she didn't pray as hard. The kind of things she prayed for was that a certain governor, or senator, or president won an election, or that someone in the rectory didn't get to serve on the board, or weren't allowed to move up to the mass choir, or as in his case, that he would give in and let her have the house. She deserved to be blessed, others got blessed always at her discretion. Never was she one seeking harmony, a middle ground that might bring a truce. No, for her there was always a loser at the end of her prayers. And any time there was a loser, it almost always meant war.

"It's cold in here," Tebby noticed right away, and this was coming from a woman who lived in a drafty, chilly apartment.

He started to put his hand over a vent when he noticed one of his clocks sluggishly flashing. He turned the light switch in his library and found there was no light. Turning back to look at the clock he remembered that the clock went to battery mode when power was lost. The dimming flashing clock meant it was losing its battery life.

"Wait right here, I'll be right back."

Sure enough the circuit breaker had tripped. He doubted that it had been a fluke because every breaker sourcing power to his room was tripped. And seeing Parker in the front room blithely watching TV irked him to be damned. He flipped the circuit breaker switches and went to the kitchen. This would fix her, pulling from his pocket the tag Roscoe had given him. He emptied the contents into her favorite drink—a diet Pepsi.

"What happened," Tebby asked rubbing her arms and blowing in her hands.

"Not to worry," and he flipped a light switch. "Let there be light…and so it shall be," looking up at the light and smiling at Tebby.

"Here…come here…" he pulled her into his arms to rub her arms and stroke her back, dosing the rubbing and strokes with a manly vim. "Just give it a minute and we'll be warm in no time." He leaned back and looked into her eyes. They were starting to tear. It was hard to believe in just a few minutes the cold had gotten to her that much.

"Are you okay? Here…let me get you a cup of tea."

"No, it's okay," she shivered. "I just think I need to get a little more sleep."

Two, three, and then four hours passed and Tebby was still sleep. She looked like a hibernating cuddly baby bear hidden beneath the mound of quilts, and the comforter he covered her with. Though when he kissed her cheek it felt as if he had kissed a sheet of ice. He stood up and watched her for a minute, her tiny nostrils flaring just enough to let him know she was getting the sleep she wanted. Perhaps he'd make her one of his variations of gumbo soup, a garnishing of vegetables he had on hand minus the shrimp doodads gumbo was cherished for. She'd need to have fuel when she woke.

The broth had just started to boil, bouncing around the onions and carrots, tomatoes and celery when he heard a car door slam. By the slam he knew it was Merda returning home from church. He parted the blinds and there she was. Draped in fake fur up to her cheeks, with a brim wide enough to hold a watermelon arrangement. She was eyeing his car, dutifully, and wasn't smiling even faintly. The war was about to begin.

Sure enough the room lost power. The broth boiled down to a feeble fizz, and all be damn it shut down his PC that he had been alternating between working on the novel he neglected for the week, and making the soup. Everything he strummed over for the past three hours was lost.

So livid he was seeing the farther reaches of human hell, he met her by the circuit breaker, breathing like a dragon and seeing like a devil at its family reunion.

"What gives you the right to be so damn wicked! That woman is sick in there! Move!" He went to grab her hand, planning to squeeze and twist on it until the rings and jewels molded into one form, except a closed fist connected with his left temple first. He felt the sting of each stone, chiseled and cut into his temple.

Blinded by pain and crazed beyond fury, with both hands he went for her neck. This was the way he would take down a drizzly he kept thinking. But the thing was,

Merda was a good foot taller than him. So instead of taking her down by the neck, he actually had a good grip on her by the furry collar. A whole lot of bear he held in both hands, so much that it was the anchor that brought her eye-level.

It was the first time he heard her scream. "Parker, help! Parker, come help me," she shrieked in this foreign pitch native to a frightened voice that sounded more like an eel in distress. A good defense method, he thought. Screaming like a neighborhood siren there was no way he could convince anyone that he wasn't the attacker. He was on his way to jail, and the worst part was, he hadn't killed her yet.

Before Parker rushed to the scene he already had let go of her, hoping to forestall prison. It still wasn't too late to say he'd been attacked first, which he had.

Things got fuzzy pretty quickly after that. In fact, the last thing he recalled was Merda's red painted nails and glitzy rings that didn't look to belong to the hardened crinkly hands, covering the breaker. The next thing he recalled was emerging from the haze feeling like the last man on earth coming out of a tunnel. Her squawking cries brought about a dozen squad cars, and three times as many police cordoning off the house as if a triple-homicide had happened. There were no sirens but there may as well as been.

The activity brought neighbors out of their homes as one police officer, an old matter-of-fact veteran with a chicken neck and nasally tone, questioned Parker. His partner, the rookie, watched over him and Merda. Others milled around the front room touching things with their eyes, and taking peeks in the other rooms.

He felt bad. He should have found another way to handle things. What it was, he still didn't know. Of all the nerve, when he looked over at Merda sitting on the opposite end of the sofa nursing her favorite diet Pepsi, she looked as satisfied as he'd ever seen her. The way she sipped the Pepsi, elaborately puckering her redone inflated cherry red lips, sticking out her pinky finger, the one partly hidden by the quartz size cubic stone, likely with a piece of his skin hanging off it. She looked like while he fumbled around in the haze, she'd been batting around freshening up for the occasion, a thought that made him sick.

It was so ugly and embarrassing. These things didn't happen to people like them. It never had before. These things mostly happened on television, the TV shows Parker watched. They were upstanding regular tax-paying citizens who went to work, volunteered in the community, put out their trash on Tuesdays, paid their bills on time, and at least for some of them, him and Parker, they stuck to their own business.

He sat there, head in his hands and rubbing his eyes, every so often peeking out of his peripheral at Merda. She could care less portentously nursing that Pepsi. And he was sure it was the Pepsi she garishly nursed because it was the only dark liquid in the frig that would require her to protect her bitter hands by neatly folding a towel around the frosty glass.

He wished they would hurry up and question Merda too, wondering if Tebby was still asleep, and warm, and how when they *took him in*, which he fully expected to happen, she would fair getting home. The minute they threw the cuffs on him he was going to tell someone to make sure she got home, likely Theresa who he saw from the window trying to get by the officers guarding entry to the house.

Plotting out his next steps, his throat swelling with each thump against his chest, he watched the veteran wrap up the questions he had for Parker, licking one finger and flipping the notepad to stroll over to Merda. He was just about to spring off the couch and tell the officers to go on and handcuff him and take him in. He didn't want to sit through the main act, Merda gearing up for a show, except she beat him to the draw. She surprised even the veteran, who sprang back as she leaped off the sofa reciting to the top of her soft-boiled lungs verses everyone assumed came from the Bible.

"Ma'am...please calm down—" The cop begged as he urgently talked into his collar. Even the rookies eyes went for a leap, two of them, and the veteran, instantly placing their hands over the pepper spray. One more sudden move out of Merda and one, or all of those canisters were coming out.

"Hallelujah! Hallelujah! Praise Him!" Merda called out to the top of her troubled lungs. "I praise him! Oh yes Lord, in your name oh dear Father, I praise him! Speak to me dear Lord! Come with your vengeance oh dear Father. Only your divine retribution can save me!"

Merda lost it. She had been in church all day, healing from the blow to Thanksgiving, trying to get *rid* of him, wasn't getting no lovin', not even from the church...and this was her claim, and now this. She'd been tested and taxed to her limit. Tried, found guilty, and convicted. She was beyond repair. Only the grace of God, a good Lord, and a fervent urgent appeal to a source higher than her could save her now.

The officers didn't seem quite sure how to handle the prayers. For a minute it seemed like they were going to ask him what to do. Asking Parker wouldn't help. He stared through the television as if they were discussing who should give a Merda a ride back to church.

Reinforcement came quickly. After all, the back-up didn't have far to travel, not lined up right outside the door and milling around in doubles and triples on the front lawn. They descended on the front room like an army blasting through a jungle. There were enough of them to guard all of England.

"Ma'am…Ma'am…I need you to extend your arms out to the side," a young female officer tried to bark. Her voice was light as Merda's, trying to reach a pitch where the oomph just wasn't there.

Merda didn't comply. She had her hands raised in the air, but it wasn't for cuffing. Dancing in small Seminole circles, moaning, crying, and calling on God Cliff had to look away. He couldn't bear watching that mountain of dark blue swooping around her, to shove her into the sofa with such force that the couch moved a few feet, and it was already up against a wall.

That got Parker's attention. The remote fell from his lap as he leaned forward, eyes opened wider than his mouth. This couldn't be real. A near seventy year old praying woman who had just returned home from a day of worship getting arrested in designer clothes, top quality fake diamonds, and real gold. Just where was her Jesus in all of this?

It was the apocalypse! That's what it was. It took her out of the house, regretful and forlorn, looking back at them out of an unoccupied daze leaning on despair. If he lived to be a billion he'd never forget that look.

• • •

He debated whether it was a good idea to go down to the precinct. Understandably Merda would be upset. He could get down there and find out she still wanted his head on a pogo stick and a platter. He could end up stuck to the end of a three-prong pitchfork going down with a dinner roll and another swig of Pepsi.

But Theresa was in his ear, "Come on Cliff, what are you in there doing?"

He was in the room checking on Tebby. During all of the shouting and praying and trying to keep power from reaching his room, the temperature had dropped down to near freezing again.

Tebby felt warmer but she was still sleep. He blew on her neck and nothing happened. He blew again and she budged slightly. It turned into a race against the clock. Should he save Merda? Or was it Tebby he cared about more?

It wasn't a difficult question to answer. Pouring chicken broth into the bubbling vegetables stewing, he went back to Tebby and got her to sit up.

"Come on Teb, I want you to drink this."

Her hands trembled as she brought the steaming cup to her lips, while behind them Theresa continued calling out, "come on Cliff, you can't let your sister rot in jail! That's your sister, Cliff!"

Running on auto-pilot he helped Tebby into warmer clothes; one of his fleece sweaters and a few pairs of his wool socks.

"How do you feel," he asked ignoring Theresa now banging on the door.

Tebby looked over at the door jumping in rhythm with Theresa's panging blows, just as serene as slow knew to go. "What's going on out there," she asked to his question instead.

He ignored her question, straightening up the socks and patting her legs. "Teb, I think we ought to get you to the hospital…"

She blew into the cup, cooling the soup by curling her lemon dropped lips and blowing against the steams dainty puffs of air. "Cliff, I'll be alright…if you could just stop that woman from banging on the door," she whispered.

• • •

Theresa was an easier contender to Merda. When he opened the door she didn't peek over his shoulder to guess what was holding him up. She chased his pupils for a flash and then brushed by him and went for Tebby.

"Awl...she's not a baby," and she looked over at him in a motherly way, "but she is a young one," and she glared at him in an admonishingly way.

Tebby sat quietly in bed, taking her time to inspect Theresa and digest what she was saying, and every so often giving Cliff the once over. Theresa thought they should get Tebby to a hospital before bailing Merda out of jail, and he agreed. Although Tebby said she felt okay, her eyes didn't hold the same sentiment. Twice, since standing over her, her eyes dipped into a nap where she almost dropped the cup.

Too weak to stand on her own, he had to carry Tebby to the car. If only this could have been the other way around, him bringing her through an archway, ready to celebrate a honeymoon. Theresa held the car door open and he secured the blankets they wrapped her in by the seatbelt.

"Terry, maybe you should drive, and I sit back here with her." His warmth, and hopefully energy would help keep her conscious.

"Okay," was how Theresa answered, and without argument she did some Theresa driving to the hospital.

Skipping stop signs, running lights, and taking side streets that had him second guessing if Theresa was as sincere as she tried to make out.

• • •

The moment he and Theresa arrived at the precinct they could hear Merda working on her wish list. She was out of cuffs and no one seemed to be listening, but Officer Tompkins (the big black officer arresting), Officer Reed (the small-voiced female officer who kneed her in the back), and several others, to include the precinct, were going to hear from her again.

"Do you mind signing here," a dreary-eyed clerk sighed, seeming delighted he and Theresa finally got there when they had. She was on her last ear, and nerve, about to call guards to have Merda re-arrested.

"It's just a seventy-five dollar fine," the clerk quietly grumbled, rolling her eyes as well.

It pained him painting things this way but it was the scene he walked onto. Merda still ranting, a nonetheless solid three hours gone by, and everyone in there either trying to ignore her, or blocking her out completely.

"Lord I'm begging you. Please show these people the way. They know not your way…you must show them Lord…help them Lord. Please help show them the way dear Lord."

"Come on Mary," that's what Theresa (and almost everyone else) called Merda. "Let's go home," and she draped an arm around her.

It was easier getting Merda in the car, but the drive home was no less painless. Leaving Tebby at the hospital without knowing how ill she was, and flinching each time Merda moved or spoke, sitting directly behind him in the back seat, made each breath he took important. Tebby could die, and he'd never see her again. Or Merda could clunk him from behind, knocking his lights out, and Tebby would never see him again.

He waited to be clobbered. His only defense was hoping she'd say something to clue him in that a clunk was to follow. He heard her behind him murmuring about Mama, the Lord, God, Jesus, but nothing about him. They made it down a ten-mile stretch of parkway, the perfect place to be clobbered and disappear without a trace, but she stopped murmuring and picked up moaning and humming old negro spirituals. Not a sound was uttered otherwise, and thankfully he made it home without being clobbered.

Things had to get better. How could things get any worse? A question he avoided like the plague thinking of possible scenarios, the most distressing being Tebby's warning. The last thing she said was she didn't want any trouble. If she learned of the spy rumor, she thus far thought he wanted to test on Pastor Edmonds, but in actuality half of Montgomery County was entertaining, he could lose her either way the story ended.

• • •

"Unck, man, I need your help…"

"Awlll…come on now Cliff, it's almost two in the morning," Jamison growled into the phone. "Me and my old lady are here in bed!"

"Unck, you know I wouldn't have called if it wasn't important." Jamison had to believe him. No one in the family who knew Jamison's bad habits ever called on him for favors, and especially not in the dead of night when his repayment fees would be the steepest. One of them could be lying in the floor in need of a ride to the hospital and he be the only one in the house with a car, and still an ambulance ride at a whopping $1000 fare was cheaper than turning to Jamison to ask a favor. It took only once to learn the hard way, a story so horrific that the mere mention of his name made the family shake their heads no.

But this was different. Tebby was really ill. An edgy emergency room doctor said she was hanging onto life by a thread as thin as angel hair. He needed a ride to Rainman, the hotel where No-No lived.

"Cliffy mannnn…ugh!" That 'ugh' was a good 'ugh!' He might have to pay for it dearly…but for the moment he was desperate.

Only Jamison could get him in and out of Rainman at that time of night, and just what were the chances of anything being opened that time of night where he could *swing by*, and leave the car running while he robbed the place?

Jamison pulled up in the driveway, motor running and engine sputtering, with him inside looking around as if someone was after him.

"Ugh, unck..." he stammered, leaning into a souped up undercover cop cruiser rushed into a chop shop and hurriedly repainted after being hustled off an auction block, "I was thinking, maybe we can take my car..."

"Cliffy...if you don't git in dis here car man!"

There was no time to argue, but he never prayed harder than the forty minutes it took them to get over to Rainman. If a cruiser pulled them over, and there was every chance this could happen, and he got arrested, as what happened to Aunt Idell on the last favor anyone would ever ask of him, he'd surely die a tragic death.

"I cain't believe you got me out this time of night caught in yo' spy business," he auspiciously huffed, plainly excited to have been chosen for the run.

Cliff kept quiet. He was a many praying man on this car ride, thinking only of Tebby lying in a cold bed, and a colder room, kept alive by ice-cold machines.

"Cliffy man...you got yo' skid on you?"

Skid? He looked down and around, and patted his pockets. What was a skid?

"Man, where's your gat!?! Yo' damn nan!?! Yo' grip! Yo' blessin' man!?!," he argued as if they were on their way to wage war, or work a robbery, where he pictured them blasting their way in and out of the place.

Cliff looked over at Jamison, concerned. He thought he had his. It was one of the main reasons he called him. Otherwise he could have gone to Rainman alone.

"You know I don't carry weapons…"

"What!?!" Jamison nearly leaped through the ceiling. "You got to be kiddin' me right!?! In yo' line of work? I cain't believe you ain't packin' no heat." He shook his head and settle back. No one went to Rainman in the dead of night minus a gun. And preferably two. Not even if they were a tenant. It was something no one did. And if they did, they didn't live to talk about it.

Something amused Jamison and started him smiling. "Man…what the hell is you up too?"

"What do you mean?" Though he knew well enough what he meant.

"I mean what the hell is you up to that you got me riding out this way at two in the morning?"

Tebby's image came back in focus. He could see her lying there, amid white sterility; the bedding, and walls, and drip tubes, and her small russet face blending into an offset haze of unspoken peace. He wanted her back. He wanted to hear her. Hear her nimble voice and petite laugh and see her eyes light up his world.

"It's this woman—" he started to explain before Jamison cut him off.

"—Cliffy man!," his uncle yelped. "You got me goin' over here for some pu-na!?!"

"No! No...it's this wo—"

And there was Jamison again, cutting him off. "—I know! I know! I heard that," and he mocked, "...it's this woman you want to see. But damn Cliffy...couldn't this wait!?! It's two in the morning! You don't know nothin' bout chokin' the lizard man!?!"

"Unck! With all due respect, please!"

"Unck...with all due respect..." Jamison mocked again, though jovially. He always got like that when he thought he was teaching Cliff something new. His eyes would lift and brighten up, and the spit would start sprouting, almost like a water fountain.

Everyone he knew, except Merda maybe, saw him as clean-cut straight type. He didn't run the streets like Jamison and many of the men Merda worshipped next to Jesus, boasting and bragging about sexual conquests, or how many bars they closed down and managed to put out of business. That wasn't none of Cliff, and none of his type of fun.

"This must be one hell of leg! Cause I ain't never heard of some pu-na that good!?!"

"Unck! This is not what this is about…so please!" This was another reason he chose not to be around Jamison for too long.

"My friend is in the hospital… dying okay…" and he let that sentiment hang in the air for a minute, "…so I'm picking up her friend to take to take to the hospital."

• • •

"Just pull in here," he told Jamison when they turned the corner to No-No's building, a tall red brick structure during the day; a mean brownish pile of rubble in the night. "She stays on the second floor…2-A."

"Man Cliff…I didn't know you got down like this," said one piped down Jamison. "Man…you done gone out and got you a hood rat!"

"No Unck, she's not a hood rat, and she doesn't stay here. This is where her friend stays," and he made eye contact. "…And she's not a hood rat either." Hoping his tone implied that No-No was a no-no to rile. It was time to get serious because night crawlers casing the hotel in this hour didn't take well to humor…good or bad, which speaking of surly, one leg out of the car and look at who strolled over to them…

...Gadoor. The man he had a run-in with the day he first visited the hotel with Tebby.

"Mannun..." Gadoor started in that street accent that matched Jamison's. "Where you been," strolling up to the car by a crooked limp, the result of street shrapnel catching him in the thigh.

"I ain't seent you in a bit," he says looking around them, as if they knew one another, but straining to get a look inside the car.

"Got sumfin for me...got sumfin I can hold...what 'chew carryin' in here," Gadoor leered, barreling into him, his chest pressed against his arm the same way he'd done the first time they met. The other time it was a lot warmer out that day. All he had beneath his arm was his jacket. And it's all that fell to the floor when Gadoor went to check him.

"Awl...you ain't got nothin'," Gadoor sneered as he stepped on his jacket walking on.

Gadoor's twin partner Lucky did him the same way. "Whoa...whoa...whoa my man...where we gon wif dis," and he pulled on his jacket, also realizing it was just a jacket. "Awl...you ain't nothing," Lucky had sneered too. "What 'chew doin' sneaking around here like this for?"

Gadoor and Lucky were two of the most notorious menaces casing Rainman, aided by dozens of clones just as intimidating. He asked Tebby how she handled going to Rainman amid all the terrorizing agents. He couldn't imagine a woman as meek and frail getting by those characters.

"No-No will be fine," Tebby told him, which still didn't answer much. No-No was in a wheel-chair. How could a woman more fragile than her keep those villains from hurting her? Those were some of the unanswered questions Tebby left him with.

"Look at you," Gadoor went on, acting glad to see him, patting him down anyway. "You lookin' like you found some money!"

"We're here to pick up No-No," he said brushing by him, Jamison on his heels paying Gadoor just enough attention not to have to introduce himself too.

"Awl mannun…No-No probably in there washing clothes or sumfin'…you know dat, baby!," he strutted off, limping and strolling away at the same time.

They got inside the building and Cliff got his first touch of Jamison surprises. He didn't know Jamison feared riding elevators.

"Unck, you're kidding me right?" How could a stick-up man with a nine in each pocket, and who'd been hauled off to jail as many times as Gadoor and Lucky combined should have been hauled off, be afraid of anything? "What, is your nine scared too?"

Jamison looked at him, holding the stairwell door open, eyeing him inhospitably. "Ha. Ha," he dryly laughed, "but I think you're forgitten who called who."

Like Gadoor said, No-No was up, but she wasn't up washing clothes. At two in the morning, Monday, she was in there playing Bid Whist. A tall, lanky, and mean-eyed man answered their knock.

"Yeah…" the mean guy greeted through the door.

Behind the man, out of view, he heard No-No asking who was at the door.

"Some knuckles lookin' for No-No," the lanky guy told her, stooping over and peering through the small crack in the door he had open.

"Well, let 'em in here," No-No chirped like her old afternoon self.

They stepped inside, the angry man looming over them from behind. No-No's face dropped when she looked up. She stared at him, and then eyed Jamison, before asking in almost a whisper, "where's Tebby?"

"Tebby's in the hospital No-No. She needs you."

Just like that the card game was over. "Git my hat and coat," she ordered to the tall lanky guy. "…And git my fixadent too!"

• • •

He couldn't have dreamt the days that passed by even if he wanted to. No-No was no Tebby by a long shot. Tebby he could have slipped in the house, quietly and undetected, but not No-No. By the time they returned to the house it was almost five in the morning. The nurse on duty that night let No-No sit with Tebby. It was against the rules, but since No-No insisted, telling the nurse she was the best spiritual healer in the country, she could both cure and strike people down, the night nurse had no choice but to step aside.

Thirty minutes later No-No wheeled out into the hallway. "Stang, you stay nearby here?"

"Not too far away," he cautiously replied, not sure if the question represented a good or bad sign. "About ten minutes away," he added.

"That's close enough. Take me to your place so I can sprucen up."

"But how's Tebby?"

"She'll be fine," No-No slung over her shoulder, wheeling down the hallway like an Olympian racer. "Ain't the first time this happened," she said, spinning around in the chair after pressing the elevator button. "She just chugged up with mucus is all. After I sprucen up some you can bring me back so we can get her out of here. Teb hates hospitals."

Two thoughts tangled up in his mind, one knotted around the other, squealing in the long echoing word, home. The possibility of Tebby getting out of the hospital was what clouded his judgment. Though he didn't understand her illness, he felt limp on one side, and numb around the mouth, but jittery everywhere else.

He started thinking how he would manage getting No-No in the house. Could he even get her wheelchair in the door? And how would Merda react?

They got back to the car where Jamison lay stretched across the back seat. It was five in the morning. Surely he was tired. But did this matter to No-No?

She flipped out the chuck-stick of a cane like one Chuck Norris and banged it against the side panel of the car. "Open up Timmy!," she yapped in what to her probably sounded like a bark, but came out more like a scratchy squeak. "This is the law," she turned around laughing, "...see, I bet that'll raise him up," which sure enough it did. Jamison sat bolt upright.

"Git this door open Timmy! This is the law!," she added on for the extra fun. The door already opened, and both he and Jamison hustling to get her in the car, she yapped like that all the way back to his house.

CHAPTER...9

The Thing About No-No, she said she never learned to read and write. She said she had never learned to sing either. And boy that's one thing she wished God had given her, a voice, which he happened to disagree with. Thank God, God thought otherwise. Of all the attributes God assigned, he would agree with anyone who said God knew His work. He assigned No-No all the right traits.

No-No came right in the house, just as he feared, banging into doors and walls, and loud. "What 'chew doin' living in a place all dis big. Stang, this place too big for one little man like you!"

Her shribbly voice, crackly but chillingly loud, woke Merda right up. She burst out of her room making him jump fearing another Merda episode. But did she scare No-No? Of course, not one bit.

No-No looked at Merda with about six twelve-inch rollers dispersed over her head, and eyes leap-frog dancing from one side of her face to the other, and started working on her too.

"Honey, I'm sorry. I didn't mean to git you up. Go on back to bed Shugga. It's just No-No. We'll git a chance to talk later in the day."

And he'd be darned if he wasn't seeing things. Merda turned right around, walked in her room, and closed the door. No-No quieted down after that though.

"Stang, why ain't you tell me you was stayin' in here with ya' mama!?!," she whispered. "How you gonna hanky pank with ya' mama in the house?"

He ignored her, quietly pulling towels from the closet and laying them on the bed. "No-No, would you like to wear one of my night shirts?"

"Now why I want to wear your things when I got my own things," and she reached around and pulled out the pad he had mistaken for a pillow. "I'ma house on wheels," she laughed. "Just let me use your washroom and you go on and git you some rest. Teb don't need to be lookin' at some bush-wacked man."

"Well, the bed is all yours I'm—"

"—and yeah, just don't you be comin' out here tryin' no funny business crawling up in it either! You see this here stick," and she shook her cane at him, "…I'll use it!"

• • •

It's the zaniest part of the entire story. All the time he spent worrying over Tebby, Merda spent muttering promises of suing the police precinct, the city, the health department, and when he stumbled into the front room, he learned she was trying to sue a doctor going by the name Dr. Blevins too.

But none of this was the zany part though. Beyond tin layers of silence and weights pinning him down, he could hear life moving around him. It sounded like Saturday afternoon noises. Lawnmowers and hedge clippers, car engines breezing by, the ticking of a clock, and the meddling of other afternoons noises that made for the best day to sleep in.

He tried lifting up once but sleep quickly hit him over the head. The third time he sprang up, crashing through both sleep and the cinder blocks. It was one of those dives off the couch where it felt like he overslept for work, the first day of work at that. Or, as if he left something simmering on the stove, only meaning to catch a few winks but caught the grim reaper of sleep and now the kitchen was in flames.

His room door stood wide open, and just as he feared No-No was nowhere in sight. A blanketed silence met his stupor as he crept out the room, fearing more what he would find when he rounded the corner. He cleared his eyes, wiping them twice before whispering, *"Good heavens, Mother Satan, meet Mother Satan."*

No-No had gotten loose. She needed no invitation to make herself a cup of coffee, unlock the deadbolt, and wheel up to the dining room table beside Merda. There the two of them were, sitting side by side, looking over a sea of papers.

He started to turn around, thinking it might be just as well if he stuck his head in the oven and closed the door. Maybe he'd meet up with Tebby in the next life.

But No-No called him back. "Good afternoon Stang! You done missed out on everythang!" She pushed back from the table, turning the chair slightly towards him. "And we need to get a muzzle for you…" she laughed at him, "one of them kinds that canines wear."

They had eaten alright, and had cleaned the kitchen to a spotless default too. On an average day Merda kept the kitchen clean, believing bleach and ammonia was the cure for all household faults, but for the trash to be neatly crushed in the can and tidied up by one cinched tight drawstring, there should at least have been a biscuit on top of the stove, or in the frig.

"Stang! You hear what these coo-coo bugs tryin' to do to your sister!?!"

Rubbing his head and swallowing hard he didn't answer. Who hadn't tried to do *something* to Merda? Someone was always out to get her, and she probably deserved whatever she got.

"Stang, these coo-coo bugs tried to pop your sister on a drug test," No-No yelled out.

Wait a minute. Go back. Rewind.

In the sweep of things he totally had forgotten about Roscoe, and the Pepsi, and calling Cathy. It was a bizarre moment. Good Heavens, it was all making sense now, remembering Merda sipping on the Pepsi waiting her turn to speak with police. He didn't want to think in spiritual overtures, but look at how timing worked in his favor. How often do these misaligned plots actually pan out just the way they were haphazardly planned? Never. He never expected Merda would grab that Pepsi, and certainly didn't expect it would be the police who would end up testing her. And strangely enough, though she looked every bit pitiful, he felt no remorse. He felt sorry for her (in a way), but felt no remorse.

At first he thought he was dreaming, and then thought he must have heard wrong. Merda looked spent and No-No didn't seem to be helping matters.

"Awl, they can't do nothing with this here," No-No argued, her crooked finger pointing on a piece of paper. "That thing got to be done by a certified testing center. Can't just no anyone take dat test! It got to have an official seal. I know! Dey tried to pull the same thing on a friend of mines…Dey had to let him go!"

Merda still didn't look elated by the news. She kept quiet staring through the papers, not even following No-No's crinkly fingers, and likely not her support either. Look at this, he gave her business to attend to, and this was that business. Looked like she was examining her life, the life she had cleaned up and put up the altar. She had to be thinking about what others were going to say about her. They saw her in cuffs being hauled away by the police, acting a plum fool. Regardless of how she proved them wrong on *those* test, and irrespective of any lawsuits she might win, the damage was done. Once a rumor got going it was hard to stop it. Something she gave little thought to when she was doing it to someone else. He still wasn't sure what to make of this turn of events, so he tried ignoring it.

"Stang, when you taking me back up to the hospital? You know we got to git Teb out of that place today!?!"

No-No epitomized an understated virtue many missed and most discounted. Her raucous voice alone could sear iron, but the wisdom she wheeled around in that one chair was enough to stop earth from falling off its axis, or knock it off its rotation at the very least.

He wanted to laugh so loud when she wheeled out of the bathroom but feared the whipping she'd deliver him in the process. Covering her head was a tweed wool hat. Beneath the hat she wore a wig, a curly wig cocked to one side, and had water lilies and little pebbly plastic looking gooseberries hanging off one side.

Before she caught him staring he turned away. There was a glass on the counter so he picked it up and held it beneath the tap pretending to be thirsty.

"Stang, would you come and git me to the hospital. You done already held us up with all ya' sleepin'!"

"Yes ma'am," and he sighed, sitting the glass down. "Right away princess!"

Swat! She swung at him with her patent leather purse, the kind he remembered his grandmother carrying to church, catching him on the backside. "And what I tell you about that!?! Don't you let me hear you sassin' me no more!"

"Yes..." and he started to say it again but caught himself, planting a kiss on her cheek instead. "Yes, No-No," he said taking hold of the chair handles.

He almost flew over the wheel-chair when he did, No-No stopping on the dime the way she did. "Stang, don't you be gettin' fresh with me either...and git off my chair! I got this...you just git them doors open!"

She was a tough nut to crack, if she was crackable at all. In that one chair it indeed held one of almost any necessity a traveler might need. Toiletries, clothes, canes that turned into clubs, a bayonet, and extra hands when she needed them. The wheel-chair was like a miniature mobile home. It even played music, reclining in three positions that elevated her legs when she wanted it to work like a sofa. An arsenal that chair was.

She didn't want much help either. "Move out my way," she fussed. "I'm sittin' but I'm no cripple," and she pushed buttons moving at a much faster clip than he could if he were running full speed.

He wanted to catch her when he saw her coming up on a set of steps, but feared getting swatted and insulted again. He watched in amazement as she took on three steps like a gold medalist gymnast. She hit a lever that jerked the chair in a backward tilt and skipped down three steps before he could finish opening his mouth to holler out.

Again he wanted to laugh out loud, watching the wig and gooseberries bouncing around, looking like a test dummy sitting in the chair. The woman was a true treat to be around.

• • •

"Why you call your sister that name? You know what that name sounds like?"

He knew exactly what the name sounded like. It was the very reason he called her Merda. "It just kind of stuck…been calling her it ever since I was a kid," he glumly answered. "I couldn't pronounce Meredith."

"Well, you a grown man now. You need to stop callin' her by that name. It sounds like murder!"

A twinge of animosity crept over him. At least he hadn't started calling her Merda to be mean, and he was a kid. Merda was a grown woman spitefully calling him out of his name.

"I guess we're even then…she calls me Satan."

"Teb, it don't bother you none, him callin' that woman a name like that?"

Tebby only smiled, more interested in seeing him sitting by her bed than she was concerned about a name she rarely heard him use anyway. "No-No, you haven't been meddlin' have you?"

"I ain't meddlin' nothin'. Stang jus' too grown to be usin' a name like that. I don't like it is all," and she turned away, really peeved about him calling Meredith, Merda.

"Cliff, the doctors say they're releasing me tomorrow if my blood pressure is good."

It was music to his ears, although he wanted to know what had made her ill. He started to ask when No-No suddenly wheeled around. "Stang, you know what an eye for an eye does!?!"

Just in that quick spin, and hearing the old axiom he heard a million times over, he saw his mother. He saw her in No-No's eyes. He was sure of it.

"It leaves the whole world blind Stang! And I'ma tell you something else it does, and you betta listen up close cause I ain't one for repeatin' myself. You'll never see a moments worth of peace you keep that bitterness in ya' heart. You've got to let it go, and you've got to let it go now! I ain't lettin' you take my Teb down with you!"

• • •

It was the jolt that sent him to Pastor Edmonds for a full confession. He didn't say as much to No-No, driving her back to her place saying as little as he could get away with, but he planned to open up with the pastor.

It was around dinnertime when he arrived at the Edmonds' home. The First Lady was just setting a plate on the table for Pastor Edmonds when he walked in.

"Oh, I'm sorry, I didn't mean to interrupt you," he started. He hadn't bothered to check the time because he was too desperate to care. No-No was right. It would be unlikely he'd get another nights rest worrying over the turmoil he caused.

Pastor Edmonds seemed to sense this. Surely he had to have heard some of the rumors floating around the church. "No, please…please join me," and he called into the kitchen, asking *the First Lady* to make another plate.

"I'm glad you did stop by," the pastor looked up, matter-of-factly speaking. "It takes a lot of courage to do what you're doing."

Suddenly he wasn't so sure he was *doing* the right thing. He was almost too sure the pastor, like everyone else, had already taken Merda's side. He could have just as well been there to tell the pastor what he thought about Merda's immaculate conception. He nodded just the same and moved aside as the First Lady placed a steaming hot plate in front of him.

As it was, the First Lady rarely attended church, although her name regularly crept in on the sick prayer list, despite being seen out at malls and in town shopping like Paris on wheels. It was widely speculated that his wife was just sick of church folks and the rumors. And really, who could blame her? There was more politicking going on in the church than what was going on in corporate and government...combined.

The front pews should be reserved for church members only, regardless of how late members strolled in. Sandals, revealing clothing, and even chewing gum should be banned. Church members tithing less than 10% should be removed from the church roster. The ministries, particularly the single's ministry and the children's ministry...should be monitored by licensed members. On and on the debates spewed. So much so that the First Lady only came to church for special events, and sometimes not even then.

But as she laid the steaming hot plate in front of him, she did so cordially, smiling faintly and disappearing into the kitchen never to reappear.

"Cliff, she needs to sell the house," he heard as his eyes dug into the lean roast beef, carefully placed beside a mountain of mashed potatoes draped with creamy brown gravy. *What did he know about Merda needing to sell the house?* Just like he thought, he had already taken sides with Merda, like everyone else.

He sliced into the beef and ignored the comment. Man was he hungry. The pastor sliced into the beef on his plate too. He watched him stick the fork in the beef and slip it into his mouth, chewing passionately.

"It doesn't have to be tomorrow, or the next day, but when you feel the time is right, I also would like to meet with you and the young lady you're seeing."

Cliff nodded, chomping down the beef. The workout he was giving his jaws did his brain good. Not only did the food quell his hunger, as he hadn't had a good meal since the Turkey was tossed up in the air, but he needed to keep his tongue going, to keep from saying things he surely would later regret.

"How long have you two been dating?"

He stopped chewing but kept his eyes on the plate. *You mean to tell him it took a big man to come to him about seeing a woman?* This was the moment when he was supposed to say he was full, and excuse himself from the table. It was none of the man's business how long he'd been seeing Tebby.

"We've been seeing each for a few months," and he wanted to ask 'why?', since it wasn't why he was there.

"That's not very long," the pastor quietly offered.

And so…

"Do you know why your sister wants to sell the house?"

And again, *no*. How many times did he need to hear it wasn't why he was there!

He mumbled instead, relishing the succulent tastes rolling over his palate. He wanted to close his eyes, and excuse himself too, butting into the kitchen to thank his wife, and maybe whisper in her ear, '*stay away from the church…nothing but bad gossip in there.*

"Cliff, she has Huntington's…" the pastor carefully looked at him, as if waiting on a reaction other than him chewing and nodding.

But there was none. The pastor was still speaking to the moon as far as he was concerned. He didn't know what Huntington's was and still didn't like the thought that the pastor had already chosen sides. No-No, and Mama, was one thing, but the pastor choosing sides was another.

He did have one question though. It was the only question he could come up with. "So, is this something you die from?"

The pastor sat back and exhaled a deep sigh. Cliff sensed he didn't care for his cavalier attitude. "The disease progresses rather slowly…even slower in your sister's case," and he stopped there, himself deciding to change course.

"Why don't you tell me what's going on between you and Meredith," he said dropping the napkin in his plate. It almost looked like a cue for Cliff to do the same, which he didn't.

The mood between them grew tense, hostile-like. From Cliff's side of the plate he wasn't getting a good vibe, not that he was doing much to change that, forking up food at a steady pace, depositing it into his mouth and exercising his thoughts via his jaws.

"Umm…" he finally said when there wasn't so much as a pea left. "You must thank the First Lady. I haven't had a meal like this since…" and he let his head drop, walking into his own trap. He didn't mean to go near Mama. But that was the last time he had a meal that lay on his tongue like the one the First Lady cooked. Mama must have been turning over in her grave seeing what was going on.

The pastor seemed to enjoy his sudden discomfort, him thinking about Mama. He folded his arms and turned his head at an angle to watch him shrink inside. *Maybe the man did have some spiritual powers.* He surely hadn't seen this precursor coming. He walked right into it, and then was blindsided.

"It's just been bothering me…all of my life she's been able to do whatever she pleases…" and Cliff ran through some of Merda's history; the whippings without mercy and whenever she felt like it, being cruel to his friends, the sexual indiscretions, never lifting a finger to help around the house, running off to Florida and marrying a bum at best, a fugitive at worse…not excluding the fact she never spent any time caring for their dying parents, still didn't pay any bills, gossiped unmercifully and hurt people daily. "Honestly Pastor Edmonds, I'm really angry and at a loss for how anyone can be this type of person and be forgiven in the eyes of God."

There was a long, long silence, and he patiently waited. The pastor had some explaining to do. He really needed to know why was it so critical that he have a cleaner heart than the one he had, while evil people with mean ugly hearts could get away with murder. Was it a matter of spouting spiritual words, as Merda did, that would ward off judgment? Perhaps he only needed to have his name added to the 'beyond reproach list'? The pastor had to tell him something, and he hoped it would be believable.

"Son..." Pastor Edmonds began...

...and he really didn't care for that tone either, but didn't want to interrupt him on such a trivial matter.

"...Accepting and serving God isn't about being good to others, helping them, and being a good person. Service to others isn't your job. That's God's job."

Not bad. It certainly wasn't what he expected to hear, though it wasn't what he wanted to hear either. All he wanted to do was get his hands on the secret code. It had to be some sort of handshake, passkey, or poncho even, something tangible that would grant him sacred access to do as he pleased and be left alone. Merda could have the house. All he now wanted was Tebby.

"Your job is to serve Him and accept His word so when he calls on you, you'll enjoy a smooth transition."

Oh man, he had better get back to church. He had missed a sermon. In fact, he missed a whole bunch of sermons. But then a thought grabbed him.

"Pastor, I'm not trying to challenge you here, but what does someone as unfeeling as my sister cares about seeing someone like me getting into heaven?"

"Cliff, I don't know what yours and Meredith's relationship is like," and he paused, "and I'm sure she's not perfect. But I know it's up to you to forgive her and find Him so that you will know His peace."

• • •

He left out of the pastor's house feeling worse than when he arrived, and this was on a full, satiated stomach too. Actually he more than felt bad. He was steamed. Livid! By the first traffic light he was thinking about turning the car around and having a face-off with the pastor. The man had pulled his leg was what he'd done.

At every red light and each stop sign he hit the brakes so hard that the car had to remind him he was taking it out on the wrong guy. *Better watch yourself…I have powers that can shut this engine down and have you using that lead foot in another way!*

Cliff had gone in there to confess, and to clear his conscience, but walked out renouncing everything the pastor said. The velvety smooth talking pastor twisted his thoughts, turned his head backwards, and had him almost believing what he no longer could remember, when all he wanted was a piece of peace!

What was all the contradictory talk about *servicing Him and transitioning?* Was that what Merda was doing? *Servicing Him,* by tormenting him? And to think he sat there nodding his head, believing in his heart that the pastor was on to something, to get in his car and find out he'd been duped. For cripes sake he already knew he wanted peace. The question wasn't what, though. It was HOW? He could never find fault with the First Lady for staying out of that rumpus, spherical talk that preached nothing. He was as bitter as he was the day before, and the day before that day.

But Tebby was important to him. If it weren't for Tebby he would have gone home to finish digging into Merda, just on the count he was that angry. Instead he went home and prayed. He asked God to forgive him if he insulted Him. He certainly believed in Him, and wanted to be right with Him. Since the pastor couldn't tell him, maybe He could. He wanted to know HOW he could right the wrongs God believed were wrong. How could he clear his conscience?

When his knees started aching, and no discernable word from God came, he got up and paced the room. He was so agitated about not saying what he wanted to get off his chest with a man who he believed was supposed to be speaking for God, that he reached for the telephone not once, but twice. He wanted to finish the talk. To say all the things he neglected to say, absent of confessing however. Confessing was no longer a consideration. He was ever so glad he hadn't confessed. It really would've bent him backwards had he confessed, only to come to that red light and see how deceived he'd been. That would've been enough to turn the car around and test the pastor's transitioning theory.

CHAPTER...10

The House of Worship. That's where No-No said he needed to be.

"Stang, when the last time you been to church?"

"Why does it make a difference? Tebby doesn't go to church."

"This ain't about Teb Stang. This is about you. You need to be right Stang. Ya' heart got to be good."

Here we go with this again. Tebby had been out of the hospital two weeks, and all two weeks, with his teeth clenched, he had been calling Merda, Meredith. It hurt like hell, and not because he was angry with her or wanted to cause her more grief, but because he had gotten so used to Merda. For some reason each time he called her by her birth name, it reminded him of Pastor Edmonds who he still felt salty about. Merda even started looked at him sideways, calling her Meredith.

"My heart is good. I treat all people the way I want to be treated."

"That ain't what I'm talkin' about Stang. You know what I'm talkin' about."

"No, No-No, what are you talking about?"

"I'm talkin' about you forgivin' people in ya' heart. What's gonna happen if Teb make you angry? You gonna walk around with that axe grindin' heart of yours, pullin' it out to chop up on my Teb?"

He couldn't believe he heard himself admitting so freely how much he loved Tebby. "No-No, you know I love Tebby. That's why I'm doing like you told me. I stopped calling her…" and he paused, gritting his teeth however, "…that name."

"Un hun…I hear you. I bet you still slippin' though ain't ya' Stang?"

"Slipping?"

"Yeah, you probably still slippin' up and callin' ya' sister murda'. You almost did it just then!"

It was true. Occasionally, once or twice he had slipped up and called her Merda. But he was trying ever so hard to get that name out of his head.

"You know what we gone have to do? We gonna have to git you in church."

"But why? Neither of you go to church."

No-No was in the kitchen, believe it or not, wheeling from the refrigerator to the stove preparing a meal that Tebby would have to eat on for a week. That's what they did for each other. When one got sick, the other would cook enough food so that there would be enough to eat between visits. No-No had her chair hiked up to the high-chair level, so that she could reach the burners and sink. Her back faced him and Tebby sitting at the table pulling stalks off corn and giggling.

Ignoring his comment she called over her shoulder, "Stang, what church does your sister belong to?"

He shrugged, trying to ignore her too. "I don't know. Can't remember."

"Stang, you know the name of your sister's church," still with her back facing them, dropping garlic cloves in a pot. "You better tell me the name of that church or I'll go right on over there and ask her myself."

He feared that was coming, and knew No-No would hold up to her word. "Tabernacle," he replied, sighing heavily and rolling his eyes.

He had been doing a lot of thinking about what No-No said. She was the furthest person from church but made better sense than Pastor Edmonds. Cliff's heart indeed wasn't right and she suggested church. Sounding like a one-time deal, it was the HOW he'd been looking for. So he decided to give it a try.

Sunday found him staring in a mirror dressed in one of the two remaining suits he had left. It was 9am, Meredith had just left, which he didn't tell her where he was going. The night before he did ask for the church's address, and what kind of services they were having Sunday, but didn't elaborate.

"Why are you asking? You never go to church," she retorted, though not angrily. She laughed when she said it. The lawsuit was coming along well. The city offered to pay for any out of pocket expenses she incurred, mostly to shut her up. Her attorneys advised her to take the deal. If she tried to fight the case in court, the city would show her no mercy, eating her alive for making them prove drugs were in her system. She really didn't want to go there, not with *those* priors. So like Merda will always be, she made sure everyone knew the city was settling out of court for an inflated sum a hundred times more than the $3000 they were giving her.

"Just curious," Cliff answered heading to his room that had returned somewhat back to his sanctuary. He couldn't laugh like Merda however, not with how thankful he was that she took her attorney's advice. Had her attorneys been any kind of thorough and found out how the drugs got into her system, he could be waving good-bye to Tebby for an unreasonable number of years.

"Well, I hope one day you find a reason to at least stick a toe in church," she hurled after him.

He had a comeback for that one, but was in no mood to challenge her. It did irk him *a little*, passing by Parker who she never charged up about not attending church. It probably was too much work for her having to kick out the wheelchair for his public appearances. But what about reading the Bible to him, or giving him some kind of church homework? She never did that either, yet he wasn't supposed to be dwelling on this. His mission was to be with Tebby.

In just that attitude he drove over to Tebby's place to pick up her and No-No. This soured him more. Driving back and forth, a sixty-mile roundtrip, about a tank of gas every other day, ate into an emaciating budget. This had to be a one-time deal. And it had to work.

They were waiting for him when he pulled up. Tebby dressed conservatively in a sensible dark wool hat and a long wool coat, and No-No dressed in what amounted to having to a double take to describe. At first glance it looked like a clump of brown rugs stuffed in a wheel-chair. The only reason he guessed it was No-No, was because of the hat, or rather hats. He remembered the last hat she wore, one of her fancy hats she said. Well this hat was two times fancier. It looked like a double-decker stacked on her head, and the deck was cocked to one side. The right side, hanging over the right eye.

"Look at Stang!," No-No near shouted loud enough to sever his eardrum. "That there don't even look like the same Stang!"

He had to admit, annoyed as he was, the compliment made him blush, though No-No flattering him, he might want to get a second opinion.

They pulled up to the church, this being after thirty solid minutes of No-No (and thank goodness for small favors), snoring, just as she wakes up to notice how large the church is. Tabernacle indeed was large. The church sat on an ample corner spreading over one full block. There were so many cars, and so much church that it took a half dozen ushers to direct traffic.

"Stang, tell them you want your car parked up front. I don't want to be stuck on no lot all day!"

His heart got a wee bit jovial then. Happily he followed the usher's hand signals pointing them into the deepest corner the lot had to offer. One, two, three, and after they got out of the car, four, five, and six cars parked directly behind them, sandwiching them in. Yes, he'd agree he needed to get his heart fixed.

"I didn't know churches can be this big," No-No said looking up at a wall of the church. "This is just too much church."

More church was inside. Oval ceiling, senate seating, and an altar set off a mile ahead of them. The more they looked around, the larger it looked like the church grew. He thought maybe they were at the wrong church. The way Meredith talked, it sounded like they were still at the old church, where a sixty-pound boy could slide out in front of a choirmaster singing in his natural voice without a microphone. Meredith must have been the spearhead behind the tithing committee.

Two deacons, friendly deaconesses, not the old ones with the tight lips and swollen noses, came right up to No-No and asked if she needed assistance.

"Yes ma'am...would you be so kind as to show me to your washroom," and No-No turned around and winked at him, "looks like we might be here a while."

That wasn't what he wanted to hear. An hour was enough church for him, and to think he thought he was being funny letting the ushers bury his car in a corner.

"How long has the church been here," Tebby asked as they waited for No-No to come out of the washroom.

"We've been in this building ten years today," smiled one deaconess. "We're celebrating our 100th anniversary. You guys are in for a real treat."

And this certainly wasn't what he wanted to hear, though his stomach begged to differ. Taking in mouth-watering aromas taunting him from a nearby kitchen he started to ask how long anniversary services usually ran, and on top of that wanted to ask if everyone would be allowed to stay for dinner. But No-No wheeled out of the washroom before he could think of how he wanted to phrase the questions.

"Look like a museum in there," No-No muttered, mashing on the chair's buttons to tip the deaconesses off that she didn't need help. Smiling like manikins they graciously ushered them up front, close enough that he and Pastor Edmonds would have no problem seeing eye to eye.

It was just about then when the hostility began to surge, rising through his veins like a cloud might clear a mountain. It started innocuously enough, No-No sitting there with her head tucked down, tears streaming over her cheeks and little hand waving in the air to a Fa-La-La gospel. He really disliked those types of songs. Why not start off rocking the house. A house of this size could really rock too. Possibly take a lot more people home in the process. Save many more souls.

The Fa-La-La gospel dug beneath his skin just deep enough to remind him how long he might likely have to endure service. His head must have been down while he was thinking this because when he looked up, Pastor Edmonds had slipped up on altar and was staring at him, fingers interlocked and if he were to describe the man's expression he would have to say not too happy looking either.

What's your problem? And he must have returned the hostile look. If he didn't, he sure meant to. He happened to recall something else the pastor said that he failed to get straight. He had mentioned something about him saving the church!?! *Was he kidding*? There wasn't a church after the National Cathedral as brazen and sumptuous as Tabernacle.

Tebby squeezed his arm, snuggling beside him as if she was cold, except when he looked over he got to see the warmest smile radiating from her face. He smiled back, probably faintly though, struggling as he was trying to suppress the surging animosity about being there. To say he wasn't *feeling it* was an understatement. He never felt as hostile about being in one place where he didn't want to be since leaving Linthicum.

No-No had to nudge him, telling him to stand when it came time for greeting first time visitors. That nudge, and then begrudgingly anchoring onto the pew in front of him to pull himself up, really hurt. Back when Tabernacle was a few hundred pews less, this would be the part when he'd have to state his name, origins, occupation, and reasons for driving 30-some miles to be preached at. But because the congregation was so large, this frill, *blessed singing angels everywhere,* was omitted.

When he stood though, he saw Mereda. Out of the fortress of choir he spotted the peacock hair and ostrich neck on the second row, also looking his way. At that point he recited a small prayer. *'God, please don't let me snore too loudly.'*

He loved Tebby, and respected No-No, but he just couldn't stomach what faced him and surrounded him. He never saw so much hypocrisy in his life. Except for Tebby, and No-No, it swam around him. The uniforms, the choir robes, the chair Pastor Edmonds sat in, and those smiling deaconesses. The chair the pastor sat in looked like it belonged to King Edward the First. The lighting for just one Sunday had to set the church back a year's salary. And the stone cold faces moving their mouths like robots to the Fa-La-La gospel made their souls feel colder than the church.

Don't ask him for a dime. They had too much as it was. And if a neighbor, other than Tebby or No-No touched him…well, they were in the right place because so help him he hoped they also spoke robotonic.

The praise dancers got on his nerves too, and the mimes he thought could use more drawing on their faces. The choir warmed up as the service moved along, but the music was nothing like he remembered it twenty-thirty years ago. Old churches used to let all souls in, including good old-fashioned floor stomping music, just in case the sermon needed a helping hand.

"Let me start by taking you back to the *Story of Joseph...*" Pastor Edmonds emitted in an abrupt jolting voice, bringing Cliff's head upright with a jerk. Nothing could have been more infuriating than looking up to see the pastor had meant to shake him up.

He was about to get on someone's case and he had no doubt just whose case that was going to be. Pastor Edmonds looked straight ahead, firing directly in his path, digging up his most profound voice.

"No!" He suddenly shouted, "This morning I'm going off topic..." continuing to fire Cliff this hard angry look. Even a few robots turned his way. Where had he been, or what had he done the other night they seemed to want to know. Even No-No looked up at him.

He took a deep breath. It was about to be on and there wasn't a thing he could do about it.

Pastor Edmonds didn't go anywhere near the *Story of Joseph*. Instead he told the story of a child seeking God by asking what God looked like.

If God was real, and everyone thought he should believe in Him, the child persuasively argued, *then someone must first tell him what God looked like.*

The robots gasped, and so did Cliff.

A few told the child God looked like a cloud. "Just look up into the sky and you'll see God," the pastor said of the well-meaning people who told the child this.

But the child was smart. He knew clouds were just clouds, so he next went to an uncle who told him God looked like thunder. And if he ever heard thunder, he'd also know what God sounded like too.

The uncle's description did not sit well with the child either. The child knew all about thunder, and knew all about the sounds thunder made too.

Finally, after asking his mother, and siblings, and teachers, and even his best friend known for not lying, the child at last went to his father.

"Papa," he says at last, *so continued the pastor*, "I've asked everyone there is what God looks like and no one has given me a straight answer yet. You are my last hope. But I'm warning you, if you don't tell me the truth about what God looks like, then I shall have no choice but to go seek Him out for myself."

Pastor Edmonds broke into the story, angry and no longer looking his way. "Be very careful what you ask for," he warned an amazed congregation.

• • •

The truth. He was embarrassed. He never meant to show that much of himself, admonishing every step he took towards the altar. *"Don't act a fool. Don't act a fool,"* was the chant he danced from foot to foot on. Lifted but grounded, the totality of eruption waiting to be born seemed to pull his natural self from his whole self as *Amazing Grace* started to play.

His relationship with God was a private matter, a delicate affair, not open for public inspection. Even if No-No meant well, her teasing him was like he had exposed himself before her and the entire congregation.

"Stang, it ain't no need to be shamed. You shouldn't be shamed of God!"

His leap getting around No-No to get at the altar may have not concerned her, but loud as she was, her shouting across the table his business, only embarrassed him more. He lowered his head and took Tebby's hand, "how's the food," he asked trying to ignore No-No.

"Don't be ignoring me Stang! What ya'll over there whisperin' about anyway?" No-No wasn't giving in. And if he didn't stop her, she was only going to get louder.

He looked across the table at her, removing any trace of unease he thought might be creasing his face. "How's the turkey? It's so tender it melts in your mouth," he nodded towards her plate, hoping to change the topic.

"It ain't meltin' in my mouth. This stuff is sticking to my teeth!"

Maybe he should have thought better of switching the topic. He turned away hoping the napkin No-No held up to her mouth wasn't to pull out her dentures. Merda walked over to the table while No-No was in that fix, busy fixing her palette.

"Finally my baby brother has decided to be a part of the family," she beamed with outstretched arms.

It was a moment when his heart dipped and the conversations around them went blank. He looked up, his mouth so full he had to swallow harder than normal. He wouldn't dare scrape up another fork full to shove in his mouth, not with every eye around the table staring at them the way they were. Namely No-No.

He hopped up and allowed her outstretched flabby arms to take him in. She held onto him, tight as he'd never known, and sobbed into his neck. Honestly, other than her trembling, beset by what she witnessed, he didn't feel much. It was the same old Merda, acting off the same old spiritual script. Once she got home, more than likely she was going to go right back to her same old ways, scoffing about the service from the opening to the closing.

*Pastor Edmonds needs to stick with the scripture...*she hated when he veered off topic, away from the Bible, not preaching according to the Word. And *did you see Sister Green...that hat was way too loud.* She hated that too, women who out-dressed her. *I knew them boys were going to act out!* She was talking about the Pastor's sons, which inevitably fed into, "I knew she wasn't showing up. And it's a sinning in a shame, too! On our anniversary! She'd better hope she don't really get sick. Ain't a thing wrong with her...and got some nerve wondering why women camp out around the pastor. The pastor needs a First Lady, not a sometime Christian!"

This was enough to get his blood boiling. The one trait that bothered him about Merda more than all of her other flaws combined. Wasn't nothing worse than an imperfect person passing judgment. Pastor Edmonds even said this was God's work.

He waited on the resentment to sprain his mood, the way it always did when he heard this tone. But nothing happened. Not this time. This time he couldn't feel a thing. No anger. No animosity. No qualms. Time is the keeper, he never did.

Other Books by RYCJ/OEBooks

Published by iUniverse

My Blackberry (2002)

Atlóta (2003)

Published by OSAAT Entertainment

the Rhapsody Series

Leiatra's Rhapsody, a *Novel* (2008)

Something Xtra Wild, a *Novel* (2009)

This One I Got Right, *a Novel* (2010)

Other books

GEM: *A Collection of Poetry, Short Stories, and a One-Act Play* (2008)

Black Table, *a Memoir/Essays* (2009)

Pretty Inside Out, *Fiction* (2009)

Storytella, *Fiction* (2010)

Tehuelche, *a Novel* (2010)

* N E W *

PUBLISHED BY OSAAT ENTERTAINMENT (2011)

Pleasure, Fiction/Erotic
A Piece of Peace, Fiction/Spiritual Romance
Rye & the Rump, Fiction/Contemporary Romance
A Blast From the Past, Poetry Collection
Mindless, Fiction/Mystery

Special thanks to all of my Readers!

OEBooks

OSAAT Entertainment, P.O. Box 1057
Bryn Mawr, Pennsylvania, 19010-7057
www.osaatpublishing.com
www.oebooks.blogspot.com